Given a Chance

The R&B Series Book 2

Olivia Linden

Contents

Playlist

Hi there ☺

I created a playlist based on the songs that set the mood when I wrote the story, and a few that were mentioned in the book for your listening pleasure. Visit my website, Queenofvibez.com for more info, or click the link below. Enjoy!

Given A Chance Playlist

Chapter 1

"I promise I will walk away and leave all this shit behind." Nicole assessed her belongings and stomped her foot in frustration. She had what was left of her life packed and ready to move to Florida, but no moving truck to put them in.

"You won't have to do that," Chelle reasoned. "Just relax. We're going to have this worked out by tonight." She perched on the back of Nicole's plush leather couch as she furiously typed away on her phone. One of Nicole's best friends since high school, Chelle was a lawyer, and the mama bear of their friend group.

"I don't want to be here if or when Trey shows up. He cancelled my damn U-Haul, so I know he's not playing with a full deck right now. I just pray he didn't get the destination address because I don't want him to know where I'm going."

Things between Nicole and her husband Trey had totally broken down, and she had been separated from him for the last year. After finding out proof of his not so legit means of making a living, she had no choice but to let things go. Especially when he felt coming home every night was optional. When the police had shown up at her door looking to question him, she moved out immediately.

Separation seemed simple enough. The problem was that they'd been together for over ten years, since she was a teen, and the emotional bond was hard to break. In the beginning, Trey would call Nicole begging to see her, and she would fold. Loneliness would play treacherous games with her mind and heart, and she would let him come over. But his inconsistency was ever prevalent, and after a while she put an end to his visits. Chelle had said it was crazy to be getting booty calls from her husband. And it was. Being denied access to her caused Trey's ugly side to develop, and he began to harass her.

Nicole had been trying to have him served with divorce papers for the last few months, but he, somehow, was always able to evade the process server. He was stalking Nicole's social media and criticizing her every move via text messages, so she decided, after her other best friend Kiko's suggestion, to move to Miami. Apparently, Trey was still able to access her credit card and cancelled the U-Haul truck she had reserved to move her things.

"Remy has a plan." Chelle jumped up and sauntered over to Nicole, who was sitting on the floor with her legs criss-crossed. "See, I told you we would have this worked out."

"I'm all ears."

"Jay owns a moving company and can arrange for a truck to be here tomorrow afternoon." Chelle's voice was filled with triumph.

"Jay?" Nicole was incredulous that the playboy of their crew could be the answer to her prayers. She stared up at her friend like she was crazy. "The most unreliable man we know?"

"That's not true, Nick. He may have been a player, but he wouldn't be Remy's best friend if he were a total piece of shit."

Nicole scoffed. "And since when does he have a moving company?"

"Since he got injured, he switched gears and started a few businesses to create multiple streams of income until he can possibly play again. He has a cousin who had a local moving business that he was able to expand to a regional operation. They do jobs all along the east coast, and even further if you have the funds."

"Are you for real?"

The thought of Jay as a serious businessman was hard for Nicole to grasp. He had been one of the star players of their college basketball team and then the NBA and had a reputation for being a bona fide player. Remy was Chelle's fiancé, and close with Jay. They both played basketball at FAMU, the college they all attended together. After graduation, he was able to make it to the NBA, playing for two and half seasons before an injury benched him. Being a professional baller only increased the stream of women vying for his attention.

Nicole, as a married woman, had always tried to steer clear of him.

"Do you want help or not? Cause you're acting a lil stank for someone who just got her problems solved by her miracle worker of a best friend." Chelle batted her eyes at Nicole with her hand on her hips waiting for a response.

"I'm sorry," Nicole blew out. "I'm just stressed and don't want any more issues. If you say Jay is trustworthy, then let's go with his company. Thank you. Tell Remy I owe him one.

"Excellent. We already scheduled the truck. And this way you won't have to leave all of your pretty designer things behind."

Nicole managed a weak nod. She wasn't exaggerating when she said she would have left all her belongings behind. She had already left behind the numerous designer shoes and bags that Trey used to spoil her with, not wanting to be reminded of the fact that they were just a tool to keep her under his thumb. A new start was something she was looking forward to, and if that meant buying a new wardrobe and furniture, so be it. Her heart had already been broken, and she didn't want any unnecessary reminders.

That night, Nicole slept on Chelle and Remy's couch. Trey was unpredictable, and she felt safer staying with her friends. She couldn't believe how her relationship had deteriorated but couldn't deny all the red flags that she had ignored along the way. Even her girl's had tried to warn her, but she wasn't trying to hear it at the time.

Famu Junior Year 2004

"Guys! I have the best news!" Nicole pranced into their dorm room with her carry-on in tow. She'd just returned from spending the weekend in New York with her husband.

Chelle glanced up from the paper she was working on at her desk, and Joey, Nicole's other roommate and BFF, rolled over on her twin sized bed to face Nicole. Joey and Kiko were on the cheer squad with Nicole, and they'd been fast friends.

"Well don't leave us in suspense," Chelle drawled, turning away from her laptop.

"Trey is moving to Florida and we're going to get a place until I graduate!"

Chelle and Joey exchanged befuddled glances as they tried to process what was just said.

"Trey is moving *here*? Wow, he can afford to do that?" Joey asked. Chelle being the voice of reason was a bit more direct.

"How can Trey afford that? Shit, how can he afford to pay for you to fly home damn near every weekend?"

Nicole shook her head and sat at the edge of her bed and took off her shoes. She was too high on cloud nine to let her girls put a damper on her plans.

"I told you. Trey has been working since I've known him, and he's great at saving money. Besides, sometimes my parents pay for me to visit. It isn't always him," she explained.

"And where is he going to work once he gets here? You know the wage difference down here is staggering, right? I get paid almost ten dollars an hour less working at the front desk of the Tallahassee Hilton than I would if I worked in Manhattan," Chelle replied.

She waited for something to click for Nicole, who as usual, maintained her perfect image of her man. A mechanic that worked on all the cars in the hood instead of an actual shop. It wasn't a far-fetched idea, but Chelle had been to his hood and seen how he was treated more like the mayor. She'd also never met a mechanic who dressed like an A list rapper and wore enough diamonds to keep Jacob the Jeweler in business.

While the girls peppered her with questions, Nicole changed out of her travel clothes and into her robe, gathering her toiletries to take a shower. She appreciated their concern, but her hubby was smart, and she trusted him. Yeah, he may have been from the hood, but he'd also shown her his books with entries from all the work he'd done.

"Well, right now the plan is to use some of the money we have saved up to get the apartment. If you guys want to move off campus, we can get a bigger place and split it. He's also got a family member here who will help him get hooked up with work, and he'll also be flying back to NY for jobs. He has it all worked out."

Again, Chelle and Joey exchanged glances but this time they both remained silent. There was no point arguing with Nicole once her mind was made up. Especially when it came to her husband.

She was love struck over Treyshawn Brown, or Trey for short. Coincidentally, they shared the same last name which she thought was kismet. They had met at Empire Roller Rink in Brooklyn when she was in the 9th grade at a birthday party for one of her cousins. Trey was there hanging out with a bunch of his friends. Nicole was a pro at dancing and skating, and made sure to show off her skills, catching the attention of Trey and his boys, who made it their job to clap or cheer whenever she passed by.

When she took a break to get some nachos and a drink, he made his move and offered to pay for her. Trey was different from the boys she went to school with. He seemed more mature, talked to her with all the confidence in the world, and wore a pair of Jordan 1s that she knew were limited edition. He was cool, and smart. They exchanged numbers, and he was somehow even able to win over her mother, who allowed him to call Nicole as often as he liked.

After that, it was a wrap for other boys. Trey made Nicole promise that she wouldn't talk to anyone but him, and she was more than happy to oblige. She bragged to all her friends of her boyfriend who was two years older and lived in Brooklyn. He was already helping his uncle fix cars at that point and making enough money to travel to Queens and take her to the movies, the mall, or out to dinner every weekend. He said that she was the prettiest girl he'd ever seen and deserved to be treated special, and each weekend she could be sure to return home with a gift of some sort.

This pattern continued throughout high school. When Nicole was in the tenth grade, Trey bought his first car. Since he had already graduated, he would drop her off to school and pick her up in the afternoons after her dance classes. That was unless he had to 'work'. His high school graduation present to her was an engagement ring, and they got married in secret that summer before she left for FAMU.

Chelle had questioned what the rush was for them to get married so young, but Nicole just thought she was jaded from her own bad experience with her ex. Her friend didn't believe or understand what she had with Trey was special.

Now that she was older, Nicole understood that he had been controlling her the entire time. Preying on her naive mind and sheltered upbringing. She learned that his uncle was one of the biggest drug dealers in Brooklyn, and Trey was his top earner.

Present Day (September 2010)

The next morning, Nicole awoke to the sound of the birds chirping. She stayed huddled under the blankets on the couch, waiting for her alarm to go off, or for Chelle or Remy to stir. Whichever happened first. She barely slept, thinking about her move and whether Jay would really pull through. Kiko had found her a place in Miami, and of course, was super excited to have her bestie move to her city. Nicole was a freelance fashion writer, so she didn't have to worry about transferring her job, but she was leaving all her family and friends behind.

She also braced herself for the possibility that Trey would show up and try to stop her. Even though they hadn't lived together in a while, he still tried to control her with his manipulation tactics. When that didn't work, he resorted to threats and intimidation. The last argument they'd gotten into before she moved out, he had grabbed her to keep her from getting her phone and keys when she wanted to leave and shoved her to the ground when she refused to let up. It wasn't the first time he had gotten physical with her, but it was the first time that he'd been so aggressive, and it scared her. Of course, he apologized and swore he'd never do it again, but Nicole wasn't sticking around to find out how far he would go.

Outside, she heard a slight commotion and checked the time. It was 8:20 am on a Saturday. It wasn't trash day, but it was Brooklyn so the noise could be just about anything. A few minutes later the buzzer went off for the front door. Nicole checked her phone for the time again, even though she had just looked at it, and wondered who it could be. Her nerves were shot worrying about Trey.

"I got it," Remy called out as he came trotting through the living room pulling on a t-shirt. Nicole watched as his tall frame disappeared through the foyer and turned the corner to the apartment door. She heard the thud of footsteps and then a familiar baritone voice greeted

Remy with the sound of hands clapping together. When he walked back into the room with Jay, she groaned internally. She hadn't mentally prepared to deal with him or his antics.

"Good morning, Princess," Jay greeted her. He sauntered up to the couch and dove on top of Nicole, his tall sturdy frame smothering her with a bear hug. Annoying as ever. Ever since they'd met in freshman year of college, he had flirted with her ceaselessly and she would rebuff his advances. They bickered like cats and dogs sometimes, but still managed to form a friendship.

She hadn't seen him since their friend Kiko's wedding the year prior, and he looked, dare she say, more mature? His creamy caramel skin had a nice Florida glow, and his deep whiskey tinted eyes were adorned with fashion aviator frames. She couldn't quite put her finger on it, but he'd changed somewhat.

"Get off me, Jay!" Nicole pushed at his solid muscular form as she ducked her head under the covers to mask her morning breath. He, on the other hand, smelled like a cross between freshly laundered clothes and a delicious earthy scented cologne she wasn't familiar with.

"Aw come on. Is that how you treat a friend?" Jay

made a show of getting up off her and made himself comfortable in the adjacent loveseat.

"Y'all could have given me some warning," she yelled out. "I could have at least brushed my teeth."

"And spoil the surprise?" Remy laughed from his vantage point in the kitchen. "You guys hungry? We can whip something up here, or I can go grab something from a diner."

"What's all this noise out here?" Chelle came from the bedroom, dragging her feet. When she laid eyes on Jay, she perked up and skipped over to him.

"What are you doing here so early?" She enjoyed the bear hug that Nicole had rejected.

"I flew in last night. After I spoke to Remy, I reached out to my team up here, and luckily was able to arrange them to be available first thing. I had to pay them a little extra, but I'm ready whenever you guys are." Jay walked into the kitchen to grab a glass of orange juice that Remy had poured and placed on the counter.

Chelle looked at Nicole with raised brows, in a silent 'I told you so'. Nicole glared back like 'So?' and rolled into a sitting position, grabbing her bag so that she could freshen up in the bathroom. When she returned, Jay was back in the chair and Chelle and Remy were gone.

"Have I ever told you how beautiful you are in the morning?" Jay regarded her as if he were seeing her for the first time.

Nicole sighed, giving him a wary glance. "At least a hundred times, Jay."

Which was true, so she had no problem with him seeing her in her headscarf.

"Well, now it's a hundred and one." He winked at her while she rolled her eyes, as usual. "It's been a minute. You good?"

Nicole pondered his question. The last time they'd seen each other, he had all but told her she needed to leave Trey. Jay had always been vocal about his dislike for how her husband treated her, which explained why he was so quick to step in and help. "I'll be even better once I'm settled in Florida."

He nodded in agreement. "I'm glad you finally made that move."

His meaning hung in the air between them as they regarded each other. Something about Jay seemed different, but Nicole couldn't put her finger on it. While she struggled with that thought, Chelle returned wearing a pair of gray sweats. It was mid August, but there was a bit of chill in the morning air. That was the crazy New

York weather, though. By noon, it would be over eighty degrees.

Nicole's phone buzzed with a call from a number she didn't recognize. Thinking it might be the movers calling to confirm their arrival time, she answered it.

"Hello?"

"So, you think you just gonna move without telling me? Like we not married?"

Nicole sighed. "We wouldn't be married if you would sign the divorce papers, instead of duckin' and dodging me!"

"I told you, we not over. I ain't letting you go."

"Trey, please. I'm already gone. Sign the papers and stop playing games."

"Ok. Nicole. We gonna see who playin'."

The call disconnected and she released a small growl of frustration.

"What did he say?" Chelle questioned, now standing in front of Nicole.

"The same stupid shit. That he's not signing the papers and he's not letting me go. Threatening me."

"What?" Chelle asked at the same time Jay asked, "Threaten you how?" He was up and out his seat, towering above Chelle.

"Not like a direct threat, just insinuating shit.

'We gonna see who playin' type shit."

"Nah. He need to be handled," Jay snarled. Remy was just walking back into the room with his wallet and shades, catching the tail end of Jay's sentence.

"Who needs to be handled?"

"Fuckin' Trey. Nicole said he won't let the process server give him the divorce papers, much less sign them, and threatening that he's not letting her go,"

"Yo, he's really trippin'," Remy noted.

"Yeah. Well, that's why I need to get out of New York. ASAP. I need to put some distance between us until he comes to his senses."

"You need me to help him get there?" Jay levelled her with a look that let her know he was dead serious.

"Thank you, but no. I don't want you getting hurt."

"Me?" Jay huffed, shaking his head. He knew Nicole would just say she didn't need the help, so there was no point in offering. Remy motioned for them to go, and he held his tongue.

"Me and Jay are going to grab breakfast. We'll eat and then meet the guys and truck over at your place." Remy explained. "What do you want, Nicole?"

"French toast?" Jay guessed.

"French toast," she answered.

"Got it chief." He saluted her and followed Remy

out.

"Thank you," she called after him before he went through the door.

After the guys left, silence settled over the room as Chelle looked at Nicole and smirked.

"Why are you looking at me like that?" Nicole glared at Chelle in return.

"Oh no reason, really. Just thinking about how fast Jay managed to get here. Like, he's taking this very seriously. He wants to step to Trey to 'handle' him. And he knows your breakfast order by heart? Seems reliable to me."

"You're a Jay supporter," Nicole grumbled. "And everyone knows that I always order French toast or waffles. That wasn't hard."

"Remy didn't remember," Chelle pointed out.

"Well, Jay's known me longer so…" Nicole wasn't trying to go down whatever road Chelle was on.

"And he looks damn good. I think even better than when we were at FAM. He's filled out a little more and grown a beard." Chelle loved to tease Nicole about Jay, because she pretended to be immune to his charming demeanour.

"I won't argue with you on that one. I think my blanket still smells like him too."

"Ah ha! I knew you noticed," Chelle squealed.

"So what I noticed? It means nothing because I will never take Jay seriously," Nicole stated.

Chelle was quiet, but they exchanged silent commentary by way of their facial expressions. Chelle's insinuating that she thought Nicole was full of shit, and Nicole's intimating that she didn't care what Chelle thought.

"Well, anyways. Jay offered to move your car, so it's up to you whether you want to fly or drive down. And as much as we'd love to road trip with you, I suggest you fly." Chelle ended with prayer hands and Nicole laughed.

"Wow, he's really got everything covered," she rued. "How much extra for the car transport?"

"No extra charge to you," Chelle replied. "We can have Kiko pick you up from the airport and you can stay with her until your things arrive. I'll also see what I can do about Trey and these papers."

Nicole sighed with relief. She was beyond grateful for her friends. They just jumped in and took care of things, minimizing her stress. She got up and sat on Chelle's lap, wrapping her up in a big hug. It was one of the rare occasions where her softer side shone through.

"Thanks boo. I was really about to run away."

"You know we got you," Chelle comforted her, rubbing her back.

"I'm so used to Trey doing everything. It took me

forever to finally plan it all out, just for him to ruin it," Nicole replied.

"Don't worry. Once the move is out the way, you'll see how fast you get settled into doing things for yourself. I'm the opposite. I had to get used to allowing Remy to do things for me, I'm so used to always handling things on my own. Tony used to complain about that too."

"I'm actually looking forward to it," Nicole sighed. She couldn't wait to be free of Trey and his craziness.

"*And* you're going to be single in Miami?"

"I know," Nicole drawled. For the first time in a long time, she was beginning to feel excited.

"I hate that I won't be up here to help you with the wedding plans, though. That's the only downside to moving away. I gain Kiko and lose you."

"Under different circumstances, I'd be pissed," Chelle replied. "But you need this, and you need to get away from Trey. I'm just happy that you're finally making a move for yourself. Don't worry about me. I'll just commiserate with Joey about being a satellite friend. My only concern is keeping Remy from kidnapping me so we can elope!"

Nicole reared her head back. "Elope? Tell Remy he better not deprive me of seeing my boo walk down the aisle!"

"Don't worry. My mother will not let that happen. Shit, neither will his," Chelle chuckled.

"How's his dad doing?"

Chelle sighed. "Since his heart attack last year, he's scaled back on the amount of time he spends at the business. Even though he is stubborn and refuses to sell it. Remy has been working to get the business to the point where he can hire some-one to manage it. Then he can focus on being an agent. Jay is considering playing ball again, now that his knee is healed and he's in better shape than he expected. He would be Remy's first cli-ent, until Shane and Dom are able to retain him."

Shane Duncan had played ball with Remy and Jay in college and was now a star center for the Phoenix Suns in the NBA, and Dom was Kiko's husband who played in the NFL for the Miami Dolphins.

"That would be so good for you guys, and I know Remy has always had his heart set on being a sports agent. I want the inside scoop whenever he decides."

"No doubt. You could even do an article on Jay and his recovery?"

"Now why you had to go and ruin the moment?" Nicole grumbled. Chelle just shook her head.

"I can't wait until you see how wrong you are about my boy. I think this move to Miami is going to be interesting for you."

"One can only hope," Nicole quipped.

Chapter 2

Despite Nicole's fears, the move went off without a hitch. Jay had commissioned four guys in total to help her. Two who assisted with loading the truck and the two who would be taking turns to drive it to Florida. He also paid for the hotel for them to rest up in and arranged for her to fly down to Florida.

To her surprise, he paid her very little attention on the flight. He explained to her that he had other business ventures in the works and spent most of the time reading and responding to emails. Nicole found herself watching him, finding businessman Jay to be far more interesting than playboy Jay. He wasn't half bad when he wasn't harassing her.

Nicole had some work things to tend to herself and went over some proofs of her latest editorial. Ever since she'd done the article on Kiko and Dom's wedding, other athlete couples had been reaching out for similar projects. She asked Jay his opinion on a few changes she was considering, and he gave her solid feedback. Even though she knew she wasn't going to be totally alone in a new city, it made her feel a bit better that Jay would be around, too.

After a while she put in her ear buds and let one of Chelle's playlists put her to sleep.

In no time at all, she sensed the descent of the plane. With her eyes still closed, she mentally braced herself for the next step in her new start. Kiko and Dom would be picking her up and taking her back to their place, and she was looking forward to decompressing. A soft caress to her nose drew her eyes open to Jay grinning at her.

"You're so cute when you're sleeping."
"And you figured waking me up was your best bet in this moment?" She cut her eyes and shook her head. "Sometimes I think you can't even help yourself."
"I have to admit that I could not keep my finger from touching your cute little nose," he replied.
"A-nnoying," she grumbled.

The plane touched down and a few people scattered throughout clapped. Again, Nicole rolled her eyes and Jay began to clap along with the others.

"Could you not!" Nicole laughed as she smacked his hands to get him to stop. "So ridiculous!"

"Why are you so damn mean?" He laughed as he tried to duck her blows.

"I'm not mean," she defended. One of the passengers in the next row gave Jay a sympathetic look and he burst out laughing.

"See? It's not just me!"

They disembarked the plane without any further incident, and even though he had a carryon, he walked with her to baggage claim and waited until her big Louis Vuitton rolling trunk teetered down the conveyor belt. He plucked it off with little effort, even as she insisted she could have done it herself.

"I'm sure you could have, but I'm here so why would I let you?"

"Good point," she conceded.

"Come one. The Sterlings await," he said as he walked toward the exit with her bag in tow.

When they stepped out into the balmy Florida air, she released a sigh of relief. It felt good to put some distance between her and her problems, and the sunny weather didn't hurt. Jay peeled off his hoodie, exposing his defined biceps and wide chest, and Nicole saw a few of the women around them gawking at him with a couple of bold one's trying to catch his attention despite him standing with her.

For all his tomfoolery, Jay didn't even seem to notice the attention, and if he did, he paid it no mind.

"There they are now," he said as he pointed at a midnight blue Range Rover pulling up to the curb in front of them. Kiko was opening the door before it even came to a full stop.

"My baby is here!" She hopped out the passenger seat and onto Nicole, kissing all over her face. Jay smirked, finding it funny how despite her grumpy nature, Nicole basked in her friend's attention. He knew that under all the eye rolls and smart one-liners was a little kitten.

Kiko and Nicole had both been on the cheer squad in college, and even though Chelle was her oldest friend, Kiko was like her twin. They were alike in so many ways, both loving fashion and dancing. Kiko had a fashion blog that, with Nicole's help, was going to be transitioned to an online magazine featuring WAGs (Wives and Girlfriends) of other professional athletes. With their access to both NBA and NFL players as friends, they had a great inside track.

"I'm so glad you're here," Kiko sighed.
"Me, too," Nicole sighed. She twirled a few strands of Kiko's hair as she admired her new style. The razor cut bob suited her fashionista flair.

Dom came over from the driver's side and exchanged a man hug with Jay. They grabbed the bags and moved toward the trunk.

"Wassup, bro? Ready for next weekend?" Jay asked Dom whose NFL season was set to start. He'd played wide receiver at FAMU and was now a first-string receiver for the Dolphins.

"I'm pumped, but I'm not ready to leave the little lady just yet." Dom gestured to Kiko who was fussing over Nicole. "How did everything go?"

"Not bad at all. She seemed relieved for the help, and Trey didn't show up, so that was a plus," Jay replied.

"I hate that I'm leaving soon because she's gonna need the support to settle in. I know Kiko is gonna be busy during the fall/winter season, and she plans to meet up with me on certain road trips."

"Don't worry. I got it." Jay stepped up to the plate without hesitation. Dom grinned.

"I know. You've had it for her for a min, man."

"Maybe," Jay said with a rueful expression. "But I can be a friend without expectations. We'll just see how things go."

"Huh," Dom chuckled. "You gonna put that charm on her, then."

"Do I look like the type to do something like that?" Jay pointed to himself like he was innocent. Dom laughed.

"Come on," Kiko called out from the car. The

women had climbed into the truck when the guys were chatting. "We're hungry. We should go to Starlight for dinner, but we'll need to stop by the house and change first."

"You coming with us, or rollin' solo?" Dom asked. Jay checked his Cartier watch. He didn't have anything planned and wouldn't mind spending a little more time with Nicole. "I guess I can hang."

"C'mon bro." Dom nodded toward the truck as he hopped back into the driver's seat.

Jay slid into the back seat next to Nicole, who looked at him confused.

"How far do you live from Dom and Kiko?"

"Not too far," he replied with a smile.

"Stop messing with my girl," Kiko called over her shoulder. "Jay lives in the building next to ours."

"Oh, I didn't realize." Nicole knew that the couple lived in the penthouse of a swanky building. She had no idea that Jay did as well.

"Yeah," Dom concurred. "You've got to check out the bachelor pad. Immaculate.com."

"I'll take your word for it." Nicole muttered. She had no plans of ever seeing his lair.

Jay just shook his head and grinned. There was something about the way she was always so adamant about not wanting anything to do with him that made him want to prove her wrong.

Twenty minutes later they pulled up to a security gate where Dom punched in a code and the metal gates parted and he drove up to valet service in front of a complex of interconnected apartment towers. Nicole followed Kiko's lead and entered the posh building. Looking back, she saw Jay give Dom a pound and head to the elevator bank at the opposite end of the lobby.

"Jay is in the other wing. Only one penthouse per building," Kiko explained. Nicole shrugged even though she was wondering where he was going.

"Why do you always give my boy such a hard time?" Dom asked, laughing at her uninterested expression.

"Cause it's in her nature to be disagreeable," Kiko mumbled.

"I don't know," Nicole replied, ignoring her friend's jab. "I guess being in such a serious relationship, watching him be such a dog was a turn-off," She explained.

"Jay was popular with the girls, I'm not gonna lie, but he never really dogged anyone out," Dom countered.

"Yeah, he was pretty straightforward about being non-committal, but most girls either didn't care or thought they'd be the one to tame him," Kiko added.

"Ok, well you guys can write your recommendation letters to Santa on his behalf." Nicole's sarcasm made Kiko shake her head, and Dom laugh.

In an hour they were back in the lobby. Nicole and Kiko were primping and preening in the reflective glass of the mirrored walls while Dom arranged for the valet to bring their car around. Nicole glanced at the tall figure approaching them and turned around to see Jay heading their way. He was dressed for the warm tropical night, wearing a short-sleeved button-down shirt, linen Bermuda shorts, designer loafers, and tinted glasses.

He flashed her a cocky grin, and she realized she was staring and resumed checking her lipstick. In the mirror she could make out that he was eyeing her from head to toe. She was wearing a simple khaki colored tube dress that complimented her warm brown complexion and her bodacious shape.

"Damn, you look good as hell," he whispered in her ear.

"Boy, move." She playfully shoved him away from her.

"Boy?" He regarded her carefully. "You know what? Im'ma let that slide. I know you've been under a lot of pressure lately."

"Because what could you even do about it?" Nicole challenged him.

"If we were alone, I'd more than show you." His voice dropped to some Barry White level that stunned Nicole from her quick comeback. Kiko cleared her throat to break up the tension.

"Ok, children. Let's play nice and have a good

night."

Jay grinned, giving Nicole a smoldering look which she returned with an annoyed glare. Before she could unleash a smart retort, Dom signaled that the car was ready.

They climbed into the truck and headed toward South Beach. Nicole took in the city's energetic vibe. Unlike New York which had a hard exterior and vast cultural undercurrent, Miami had a bold passionate feel to it. The vibrant colors, mix of cultures, and historic relevance resonated with her soul. Her excitement was building, and she could feel her creative juices churning.

It didn't take long until they pulled up to the Art Deco inspired restaurant. Kiko loved Starlight because they served Japanese brunch all day, and Dom enjoyed their ribeye steak. What she loved most, though, was their karaoke after dark. She couldn't sing to save her life, but she loved trying and embarrassing the heck out of Dom with her serenades.

They all enjoyed drinks with dinner and caught up on what they were each up to. Nicole seemed to be the only one that didn't know the various things that Jay was involved in. She just knew that he played two years in the NBA before injuring his knee. Apparently, he was working out with a few teams to see if he was in good enough shape to return to the league. It was like she was really seeing him for the first time.

Kiko had just returned to the table after a gravelly rendition of "Who Can I Run To" by Xscape. She was pumped up by the support and cheers from the other sub-par singers in the restaurant.

"Jay! Are you going up?"
He was casually sipping his drink and people watching, enjoying the scene.
"Nah," he declined.
"Come. On. You have to do Babyface. Please?"
Kiko even threw up her prayer hands, pleading with her eyes. Jay looked from her to Dom, and then to Nicole. A sly expression came over his face as he accepted.
"Ok. Fuck it."

He took one last sip of his drink, winking at Nicole before striding toward the DJ booth. They exchanged handshakes and he proceeded to select his song of choice.

"Jay is so good," Kiko droned. "He usually does When Will I See You Again. Sounds just like him!"
"I'm startin' to feel some type of way about this."
Dom pouted at his wife who planted a big kiss on his cheek, just to wipe off her lipstick smear.
"I can't wait to see this," Nicole quipped as she sipped on her mojito.

There was a moment of silence as Jay grabbed

the microphone off the stand and then the music started. Staring right at Nicole, he began.

"Hey, come here for a second," he said in a smooth, hushed tone. "I don't like the way he treats you. He doesn't deserve you. He really don't."

Jay then launched into a sexy rendition of "Soon As I Get Home" by Babyface. The crowd whooped and squealed as he pandered to different ladies. You would have thought he was the actual artist the way they were reacting to his performance, singing along with him as he broke into the chorus. He had a little pitch issue, but his voice was panty dropping smooth.

"I give good love. I'll buy your clothes. I'll cook your dinner too. Soon as I get home from work." Nicole was dumbstruck as she followed Jay with her eyes while he worked the room. His voice was melodic and mesmerizing, raising his normal baritone pitch to a high tenor. Of course, his looks were a huge draw. A tall, muscular man with a body that screamed athlete, with tattoos that stood out on his light brown skin. The way he crooned the lyrics with a sensuality and vulnerability could probably disarm any woman in his orbit.

Kiko nudged Nicole with her shoulder and whispered, "Told you he was good."

Nicole couldn't even front, and nodded in agreement, never taking her eyes off him. His song choice was clutch, and she wondered if there was a special message. Her question was answered when he strolled toward her, taking her hand in his as he began the second verse.

"It doesn't make sense. That you should have a broken heart. If I were the only one. I'd never let you fall apart."

Nicole tried to convince herself it was all part of an act, but the sincerity in his expression was unnerving. She grinned as he continued to serenade her, secretly enjoying the envious glances from the other women. When he kneeled in front of her and belted out, *"Girl, I'll treat you right, And I'll never lie or flirt. For all that it's worth, I give good love..."*, she averted her eyes and shook her head to conceal the fact that she was blushing.

Jay rose to his feet, caressing her cheek with his finger before moving back toward the center of the dance floor and finishing out the song, maintaining eye contact with her as the lyrics continued to promise a faithful lover who would take care of her.

Even Kiko and Dom were singing along with him by the end.

When the music went off, he received monstrous

cheers and catcalls from the ladies in the crowd. Surprisingly, his response was modest, throwing an almost shy wave as he mouthed thank you to the audience. When he walked back over to the DJ to give him a pound, he was approached by a tall dark-skinned beauty who looked like she could have been a spokesmodel for apple bottom jeans.

"That's that player shit," Dom chortled to Kiko as they observed his unnaturally humble disposition.
"Ok," Kiko tittered in agreement. "They were damn near throwing panties at his ass, and he's acting like Stevie Wonder."

Nicole joined them in their laughter even though internally she was admonishing herself for being annoyed that he was still over there flirting and hadn't returned to their table. Finishing her drink in one long gulp, she contemplated how to let Kiko know that she was ready to leave without being a party-pooper.

"Ready to hit the road?" Kiko gave her a knowing smile. Nicole sighed and smiled back, stifling a yawn.
"Ok, ladies. Allow me to escort you to our chariot," Dom announced in a terrible British accent. Pushing away from the table, he offered his hand to help them out their seats.
"You are just the cutest," Kiko gushed as she

scrunched his cheeks. They made a striking couple. Both a creamy chocolate brown; Dom tall and covered in ink starting from his days running the streets, and Kiko with a fit, slim-thick frame.

Dom motioned that they were leaving to Jay who threw his hands up and mouthed 'already?', to which Kiko pointed to her watch. Jay nodded and waved but didn't leave his conversation. Nicole gave him a slight wave and he acknowledged her with a nod and wink.

"Jay is a fool," Kiko said.
"He's good people, though," Dom noted.
"That he is," his wife agreed.
"Mmhmm," Nicole replied. "And he has no problem spreading his goodness around."

"That's single life for you," Dom lamented as they headed toward the exit. Kiko shoved him on the shoulder and rolled her eyes. "You sound like you're missing out, or something."
"Nah," he replied, pulling her close. "Are you crazy? Look who I'm going home with."

Later that night the girls sat in Kiko's movie room sipping on wine and reminiscing.
"Girl, I knew you were going to be my friend, immediately," Kiko prattled. "When I saw how you killed that routine when we auditioned for the squad, I was like 'oh, a bitch that can keep up with me' finally," she laughed and sipped her

pinot noir.

"Keep up with you?" Nicole laughed. "Girl, you know I could have been the leader of the squad if I wanted it. I was just fine showing off my skills, no title necessary."

They both laughed and fell into a comfortable silence as *Boomerang* played on the theater screen. It was one of their favorite movies to watch together. Nicole sighed as she leaned back in the plush leather recliner, and then her phone dinged with a text message.

```
Jay: I was looking forward to you singing to me
Nicole: Ha! Maybe next time
Jay: Promise?
Nicole: Maybe
Jay: You will
Nicole: Bye Jay!
Jay: Sweet dreams Love
```

Nicole paused for a moment, caught off guard by his last message. She found herself smiling and shook her head to snap out of it, tossing her phone to the side. When she looked up her friend was watching her in amusement.

"So, Karaoke was fun," Kiko said, wagging her eyebrows suggestively. Nicole looked over at her and grinned.

"It actually was. Thanks for suggesting it. My plan was to lay up in the bed."

"Oh, no." Kiko looked at her like she was crazy and shook her head. "I'm not letting you mope around. I know that's what your ass been doing."

Nicole couldn't even argue with her. "I know. I just feel so lost. Like, what am I even supposed to do next?" She looked to her friend in earnest and Kiko gave her a small smile.

"You take it one day at a time. And you let your friends take you out, even if it's silly shit like Karaoke."

"Im'ma need you to work on your tone a bit if you want me to ever go with you again," Nicole teased, putting a finger to her ear like it was aching.

"Whatever, you didn't seem to mind when Jay was *sanging* to you," Kiko snickered as she re-enacted Jay kneeling in front of Nicole.

"And here you go," Nicole chortled. "Don't even start!'

"Oh, I'm gonna start!" Kiko jumped up and shook her finger. "You think I didn't peep you?"

"Peep what?" Nicole folded her arms across her chest.

"Don't give me that. I know you Ni-cole. I saw how you was ogling my boy. You enjoyed that little performance."

Nicole shrugged. "It was cute. I don't know why you're making a big deal."

"I'm just calling your snarky ass out because you always act like Jay has some sort of incurable illness that you don't want to catch."

"The verdict is still out," Nicole snipped.

"Shut up," Kiko laughed. "You seemed ready to catch everything he has when he said he gives that good, good love and looked deep into your pretty brown eyes!"

"You're so damn extra. What are you doing?" Nicole took a long sip of her wine while Kiko stared seductively into her eyes.

"This," Kiko said, and winked, "is how you were looking at Jay when he was on his knees."

Nicole sputtered, throwing a hand over her mouth to prevent red wine from spewing everywhere. She choked down her sip and gasped for air as she giggled. "What is wrong with you?"

Kiko continued with her shenanigans, rolling her eyes around like she was cross-eyed before falling into Nicole's lap.

"Dom!" Nicole called out, even though she knew he couldn't hear her. "Come get your wife!"

"Yeah, Dom!" Kiko mimicked. "Come in here so you can tell Nicole how you saw her drooling over Jayshon Errol Montgomery."

Nicole covered Kiko's mouth to shut her up. "Will you stop?" Giggling, Kiko put her hands up in surrender and Nicole relented. "Errol, though?"

"I think he's named after his Jamaican grandfather or uncle or something," Kiko explained.

"Oh," Nicole replied. "I didn't know Jay was Jamaican."

"That's right, your daddy is too. Look at y'all, matching."

"Kiko. Please."

"I'm saying. Jay is fine as hell. What's wrong with admitting that?"

"Jay is fine as hell," Nicole repeated in a mono-tone voice. "Satisfied?"

Kiko grinned. "I think you would be if you let him hit."

"Let him hit? Nicole pushed Kiko off her lap and got up. "Now I know you're trippin'. I'm going to bed."

"*I give good love...*" Kiko sang as Nicole threw up the middle finger and left the room.

Chapter 3

Nicole slept in the next morning, feeling secure for the first time in months. The amount of relief she felt not worrying that Trey would come knocking on her door was immense, and she realized how much stress she'd really been under. She had always been the 'sassy' friend out of the crew, but being classed as grumpy more than a few times had really struck her.

She couldn't remember the last time she felt happy and carefree, and as corny as karaoke had been, it was the most fun she'd had since the wedding. Moving closer to Kiko was something she'd always wanted to do, but Trey wasn't trying to leave New York permanently. Even when he had moved down to Tallahassee to live with her until she graduated, he had spent more time away than with her.

Why had it taken so long for her to see what he was doing? He had been controlling her since she was fourteen years old. His swag and street demeanor had charmed her into accepting his way of doing things. He was older, more experienced, and cooler. Everything that appealed to her shallow teenage fantasies. Trey even had her mother and father fooled because he presented himself as so responsible and mature.

Being able to say she was engaged in high school? She had flaunted her ring around like she was 'The Queen of Sheba', or so her mother had said. Her pride and ego had been so off the charts. When he suggested they run off and elope, Nicole felt like she was swept up in a whirlwind. To her, Trey loved her so much he wanted to 'lock her down' before she left, not even considering that he was just trying to prevent her from meeting someone new.

Her text message notification went off and she pulled her phone off the charger.

```
Jay: Good morning
Jay: Good news. Truck will be here this evening.
Nicole: Great news!
Jay: I'll text you when they're
about an hour out.
Nicole: Ok. Thank you!
```

That really boosted her mood. As much as Nicole loved her friends for letting her crash, she couldn't wait to sleep in her own bed in her new place. It was crazy that she hadn't even seen it in person yet, but as soon as Kiko returned from her pilates class, they were going to get food and head to Target to get a few things she needed. Then they'd head to the house to clean and prep for the movers.

The initial excitement she felt the day before with Chelle was stirring and growing within her. There were so many things that she had wanted to experience that she had denied herself or pushed out of her mind. Jay being one of those things. Yes, she didn't like that he was a player, but there were other reasons she kept him at bay.

2005 Spring semester freshman year

It was the basketball team's last game of the regular season and they had made the playoffs, so of course there was a huge party. All the girls on the cheer squad dressed up in their special uniforms to support the guys. Kiko and Nicole were notorious for choreographing extra routines for them to do at parties, which gave them a huge buzz. With Nicole's killer body, she had guys flocking to her, until word got out that she was *taken* taken. The only person who dared to flirt with her was Jay.

The party was thumping' and everyone was having a blast. Even Chelle had shown up and showed out with the girls on the dance floor.

Her and Joey were having a dance-off to TLC's Ain't Too Proud To Beg when Nicole snuck off to call Trey. He was upset with her for not coming home that weekend, for a stupid party, as he called it. She tried to explain to him that it was a big deal for the team, but he wasn't trying to hear it. He hadn't called her all day, and wasn't answering her calls, but she kept trying.

Slipping into one of the unoccupied bedrooms of the frat house, she pulled out her phone. Still no word from her husband, but she called him anyway. This time, he actually picked up, but all she heard was loud music and chatter in the background. Then she heard a female voice say 'Your phone was ringing' before muffled talking and the call disconnected. Her heart sank into the pit of her stomach, and she felt a blind rage brewing inside. She called him again, but this time the call went to voicemail.

Nicole must have called him another ten times before she accepted the fact that he was not going to answer her. She kept replaying the girl's voice in her head over and over again. That prompted another phone call that included a scathing message, and then she sank down into a defeated puddle on the tattered rug. She fought to get her breathing under control, and didn't want to cry, but the more she tried not to, the more the tears came.

"I know where you keep your stash at," a voice boomed outside the door right before Jay came barging in. He took one look at her, crying on the floor, and the smile on his face dissolved. Closing the door, he came over and squatted down to her level.

"Did somebody hurt you?" The question was laced with concern and barely suppressed anger. "No, Jay," she sighed. "I'm fine. Nobody touched me."

"So why are you crying?" He tipped her chin toward him, searching her face as if he could find the answers somehow. Nicole, afraid her voice would betray her, just shook her head. Then her phone dinged with a message, and she gasped.

Hubby: Why don't you enjoy your party and stop blowing up my phone. You didn't want to spend time with me, so I'm busy.

Nicole stared at the message, and she felt sick. Was he insinuating that he was cheating on her, or was he just trying to piss her off? Jay snatched the phone out of her hand and read the message.

"You're man text you this?" The disbelief in his voice made her feel even worse.

"Just give me my phone back and don't worry about it." Nicole tried to snatch her phone, but he held it away from her.

"This is not ok. You know that right?"

"He's my husband, Jay."

He grasped her chin, glancing between her enchanting eyes and full lips. The air between them was charged as they regarded each other. Jay wasn't a pretty boy, but he was handsome. Fine. There was something about him that made you want to know more, and Nicole felt something stirring inside her just being near him.

"I don't care who he is. No one should ever talk to you this way," he said as he held up her phone, flashing the ugly text. Nicole just nodded.

Grabbing her hand, he stood back up, pulling her up with him. She was a bit wobbly, and he steadied her. Nicole braced herself, placing both hands on each of his strong arms. She took a few deep breaths, preparing herself to rejoin the party.

"You gonna be ok?"
"Yeah, I'm fine." She gave him a small smile and he pulled her in for a hug.
"I ever see you crying again and Im'ma kill that muhfucka."
"Ok, Jay," she chuckled, but he wasn't laughing.
"You so damn beautiful," he drawled, his voice dropping so low it sent shivers down her spine.

 He leaned in and Nicole closed her eyes, reflexively, breathing in the scent of his dark chocolate cologne. When all he did was kiss her on the cheek, she smiled to hide her disappointment. Taking her phone out of his hand, she left him to retrieve whatever stash he'd come in the room to get.

Present

The day passed by in a blip. By the time the girls finished brunch it was well into the afternoon. Nicole knew it was a bad idea to order the endless mimosas, but Kiko insisted it wasn't brunch without them. Then Dom and a few of his teammates showed up and it turned into a mini party. Nicole had the feeling that it was also Kiko's plan to present her with eligible bachelors.

After that, they had gone to Target, tipsy, and picked up way too many things that she didn't need. Another thing they had in common was their love of shopping, and retail therapy was Nicole's favorite pastime when she was anxious or stressed.

When they finally made it to the house she was renting, Nicole was bristling to get inside. It was a quaint two-bedroom garden style home in a fairly new subdivision in North Miami, one room serving as her home office slash guest bedroom. She also wasn't too far from Kiko's apartment building, which was a huge plus.

They spent the rest of the afternoon drinking more mimosas, and cleaning. Kiko brought her big speaker, and they blasted songs from their high school and college days. When Freak Like Me by Adina Howard came on, Nicole really cut up. Even though she'd only been with one man, she definitely considered herself a freak and had a whole list of things that she wanted to do but hadn't yet.

Of course, she had a provocative routine for the song that had almost gotten her and Chelle kicked out of their eleventh-grade talent show. Kiko demanded she teach her the steps after hearing the story, so Nicole began the moves while she sang the lyrics.

She was dropping it like it was hot when Jay, bopping his head to the music, came strolling into the kitchen where they were supposed to be cleaning the appliances. Kiko screamed at his sudden stealth appearance and Nicole flinched, causing her to lose balance and fall backwards as she cried out, "Jesus Christ!"

Jay paused with his hands up, trying to hold in his laugh as the girls regained their composure. When Kiko began to giggle, Nicole snorted, and they all burst out laughing.

"You scared us half to death," Kiko chortled with her hand on her heart.

"Maybe next time don't leave the door unlocked," he suggested as he held out his hand to help Nicole back on her feet. On purpose, he pulled a little too hard causing her to fall against him. The jolt of electricity from their body-on-body contact shocked them both.

Nicole snatched her arm away and cut her eyes at him, as usual, pretending it didn't affect her. Jay was quietly observing her, and when his eyes lingered on her chest, she glanced down to see her nipples rock hard and poking through her tank top. She felt a flood of heat spread throughout her entire body with an epicenter between her legs. Turning away, she grabbed the orange juice out the fridge to pour herself another drink.

"Want one?" She waved the champagne and orange juice bottles toward Jay who declined.

"I'll pass. I want to be sober when the truck comes."

"That's smart," Kiko pointed out. "Smarter than us. We been drankin' since early."

"Wow. I wouldn't have suspected a thing if you hadn't told me," Jay replied, but his expression said otherwise.

"I thought you were gonna tell me when the truck was on the way?" Nicole asked as she swirled her drink like it was a fine wine.

"Well, I was and then Dom said you guys were here already, so I decided to come by instead."

He turned his hat backwards and leaned up against the counter. The way his triceps flexed when he folded his arms across his chest made her do a double take. Nicole thought she might have to take Kiko up on the offer to hook her up so she could stop looking at Jay like a chicken dinner.

"Hey, don't mind me," he said. "Y'all can get back to bussin' it wide open or whatever was happening before I walked in."

"The moment has passed," Nicole said as she sipped her drink.

"Maybe next time." Jay looked at her expectantly.

"Maybe," Nicole shot back.

"Promise?"

"Ok... What am I missing?" Kiko looked between them, confusion and intrigue written all over her face.

"Not a damn thing," Nicole scoffed. She put her glass down and resumed cleaning the shelves for the fridge.

"Well," Jay said as he hopped up on the kitchen counter. "Your stuff is about twenty minutes out."

Nicole paused from scrubbing. "That was mad fast."

"Yeah. They probably didn't stop for too long. If you have two guys that don't mind driving long hours, they can each knock out about twelve to fourteen hours a day. I know I'd rather spend the night in Miami than South Carolina."

"That makes sense," Kiko slurred.

"Damn. How much have y'all had to drink?" Jay noticed the empty bottles for the first time.

"Enough," Nicole said at the same time Kiko replied, "Not that much."

He laughed. "Right."

"I'm just here for moral support, really," Kiko commented.

"Lucky for Nicole, me and the guys can get everything squared away in no time."

Nicole's head whipped toward Jay. "*You* and the guys?"

"Yeah," he shrugged. "I help out if needed. We'll set up anything that needs putting together and place them wherever you want. It's a full-service operation."

"That's what I'm talking about." Kiko raised her almost empty glass toward Jay and then downed it.

Nicole didn't say anything. She was too busy grappling with whatever reaction her body was having to thinking about Jay putting his muscles to use. For years, she'd had an excuse to ignore him and keep him at arm's length but spending time around him and learning things about him, she found her interest thoroughly piqued. And her hormones.

Just about the time the girls had finished their cleaning, the rumble of the semi-truck alerted them that the movers had arrived. Nicole actually clapped her hands in excitement as she skipped toward the front door. Jay was already outside, directing the guy who was driving on where to park.

An hour and a half later, all her things were placed, and Jay was putting in the last few screws for her dining room table. The other guys were sipping on cold waters, and Kiko was sprawled across the couch trying to sober up. Nicole thanked the movers profusely for being so efficient and grabbed her purse to give them a tip. Jay put out his hand to stop her, taking her purse and placing it back on the table.

"I got this." He walked the guys outside and gave them each a generous reward for a job well done. He also sent Dom a text letting him know he needed to come pick up his wife.

After the couple went home, Nicole and Jay were left sharing the remainder of the champagne from earlier. She was lounging on her couch, and he was sitting on the floor with his back propped up against her legs.

"You know, I was expecting way more stuff. Where are all your bags and shoes?"
In school, Nicole was known for her extensive sneaker collection, featuring various styles of Jordans, and her bags. Trey spoiled her with designer bags, always buying her the latest releases.
Nicole sighed. "I didn't want anything that reminded me of Trey. He bought all that stuff, and knowing what I do now, I don't want any off it. It's a reminder of how dumb I was to think he

could afford half of the lifestyle we had."

"Don't be so hard on yourself," Jay said. "There's nothing wrong with trusting someone, and you were young and over a thousand miles away. He could have been doing anything, and you wouldn't have known."

"I guess. Even with my scaled back belongings, I still can't believe this went so well," she sighed in relief. "Thank you."

Jay nodded his head. "You're more than welcome. Just glad that I was able to handle things."

"And your guys were great. I'm very impressed."

"I think that's supposed to be a compliment," Jay said as he looked over at her.

She laughed. "No, I mean it. I know you said you're a businessman now, but it's different seeing things in action. Remember, for four years I only ever knew you to dribble a ball and hook up with half of the female student body."

"We all have to grow up at some point, Nicky."

"Nicky?" She glowered at him, putting one finger up. "No. Absolutely not."

"What?" Jay chuckled. "I can't call you that?"

"Again, I say, no."

"I don't know. I kinda like it." For some reason, Jay enjoyed her visceral response to his nickname for her.

"Jay, if you ever call me that in front of anyone, I will kill you!"

"Ok. Fine. It'll be just for us," he murmured huskily, winking at her.

"Get out." She nudged him with her knee as she swung her legs off the couch. "Get out of my house, *now*."

Jay laughed but put his hands up in surrender. He grabbed the empty bottle and glasses and took them to the kitchen as Nicole followed behind him, fussing. "I don't need you to clean up, just take your crazy ass outta here." She snatched the glasses from him, placing them on the counter and redirected him to the door.

"Five minutes ago, you were complimenting me and now you're kicking me out," he chuckled as she unlocked the door.

"Yeah, well when you start with your foolishness, that's where I draw the line." She pushed him in the back as he neared the entrance, but he turned around and placed his hand on the door over her head before she could close it in his face. Moving toward her, he tilted his head and grinned.

"I think you're forgetting something." The way he stared her down caused goosebumps to ripple over her flesh.

"What's that?"

"Don't I at least get a hug for my services?"

Nicole narrowed her eyes, shooting him a suspicious glare. She *was* thankful and had given all their other friends hugs for helping her out, meanwhile he'd come through for her the most.

It was Jay though, and she was almost certain that he had an ulterior motive. Still, she stepped toward him, and he opened his arms for her to walk into his embrace.

She snaked her arms around his waist, and he closed his around her. Jay squeezed her closer, the scent of cedar and sandalwood engulfing her, but he didn't do anything inappropriate like she had expected. The longer he held her, the more she realized how much she needed a good hug. When he placed a gentle kiss on her forehead and pulled away, she wasn't quite sure why she felt the urge to pull him back. Fighting the impulse, she smiled instead.

"Thanks again. You're a lifesaver." She put her hand up for a high five and he smiled down at her and smacked his palm against hers.
"And don't you forget it." He shot her a wink and turned away. She watched him walk down the path toward his car wondering what was happening to her, and how Jay was managing to get in her head.

"Make sure you lock your damn door," he called out before getting into his sleek Bentley coup.

Nicole gave him the thumbs up and did as he said. She looked around her new place and felt a surge of emotion overwhelm her. Tears sprang to her eyes as the enormity of her situation finally settled in. She slid down her front door, sitting with her back against it, and cried for what was no longer.

Chapter 4

With each passing day Nicole felt better about her decision to move. The weather was incredible, and she took advantage by getting outside every day to enjoy it. Granted, usually either early in the morning or in the evenings when the sun wasn't beaming and attempting to dehydrate her soul. Of course, Kiko was obsessed with taking her everywhere and showing her all that south Florida had to offer. Nicole, however, had to draw a line at gator tours in the Everglades.

The only thing that was getting to her were the random bouts of loneliness. Even though she had been separated from her husband for a while, moving to a new state seemed to emphasize her single status. In New York, she had her family and friends to visit and keep her company. While living close to Kiko was amazing, she couldn't monopolize all her time. Kiko was an NFL WAG and personal stylist. Her hands were full with different events, plus her clientele was growing.

Of course, there was Jay, who had checked in with her a few times, dropping off a list of handymen and important numbers to have, and doing manly things around her place that she wouldn't have thought of, like checking her HVAC system. He'd noticed that the screens on her windows were flimsy and made it his duty to replace each one. Other than that, he didn't hound or bother her like she feared he would. She could see why Chelle said he was such a good friend, even though she hated to admit it.

Kiko alluded to her softening toward him one Saturday at brunch. "So, I see you haven't killed Jay yet."

Nicole slowly chewed her breakfast burrito as she eyed her friend. She was always on alert whenever his name was brought up. Kiko laughed and continued her observations.

"I like how he took care of securing your windows. That was nice of him to do."
"Yes, it was," Nicole deadpanned after sipping her mimosa.
"Have you guys gone out or anything?" Kiko decided to rephrase her question after Nicole

scoffed at her. "I meant, like for breakfast or dinner. Things like that. Friend things."

"Just stop," Nicole chuckled, putting one hand up. "And no. We haven't gone anywhere together or done any friend things. I'm not trying to send the wrong signal."

"Hmph," Kiko mumbled as she nibbled her croissant sandwich.

"Hmph, what?" Nicole knew her friend was on some foolishness, but she went along with it.

"I mean, you gone have to keep yo damn eyes closed around him if you ain't tryna throw no signals." She sipped her own drink, exaggerating her thirst.

"What does that mean?"

'It means," Kiko said, code switching to sounding like a flight attendant, "that your mouth says one thing, but your eyes say something else. If you don't want to give the impression that you're into him, then work on not eye-fucking him all the time."

"You play entirely too much," Nicole muttered.

"I wish I was, but I'm being dead serious. I don't know why you act like you're not attracted to that man."

"Just because I find Jay attractive, doesn't mean I have to date him or want to fuck him," Nicole opined.

"True," Kiko agreed. "But why not? You been with Trey since Moses was a lad. I know you're ready for something different."

Nicole looked to the sky to keep from cracking up. "God? Why did you send me this looney toon?"

"I'm saying," Kiko giggled. "You've got one of the most sought-after men in Miami ready to serve up his pro athlete physique on a silver platter and you're acting like someone offered you dog food!"

"I'm gonna pray for you." Was all Nicole was able to say while trying to muffle her cackling from the restaurant's other patrons. When she finally recovered, she shook her head. "I just don't want anything messy. I don't want nobody calling me bout they man or coming to me as a woman. I just want to get my back blown out from time to time. Maybe a cute date here or there. But not Jay. I'd rather explore one of the other pro athlete selections that you've provided."

"So, no Jay?" Kiko wasn't sold on her friend's explanation and wanted to be clear that he was off the table, so to speak.

"No Jay," Nicole reiterated.

"Ok, so in that case..." Kiko bounced in her seat as she picked up her phone and started scrolling. Nicole smirked, patiently waiting on her friend's pending mischief.

"How about Deshawn?" She handed the phone over, showcasing a picture of a bulky teddy bear of a man with a beautiful smile and dreads. "Or..." She leaned over and swiped to the left. "Vance?"

"Why not both?" Nicole grinned, and Kiko

sucked her teeth.

"No, Miss 'I don't want any mess'. They're friends, so you have to pick one."

Nicole hummed as she slid back and forth between pics. Where DeShawn had a big smile, Vance gave the camera a look like he just knew he was fine. Cocky.

"I'll go with DeShawn," she decided.

Kiko tilted her head as she examined both pics again. "What's wrong with Vance?"

"He looks a little full of himself. Am I wrong?"

"No," Kiko chuckled. "You're not wrong, but he's a cool guy. Dom has known him for years. I think they played pee wee football together."

"Aww, that's cute. DeShawn, please."

"Ok," Kiko conceded. "DeShawn it is. I've never met him, but when I asked Dom for the single guys without drama, he named these two.

"I hate having to blind buy," Nicole joked.

"I have an idea!" Kiko's eyes widened, and Nicole squinted in suspicion.

"I don't know if I should be excited or afraid."

Kiko brushed off her snark and launched into her plan instead. "The team has their bye week and are off next weekend. I can throw a little get together and have a few people over. We do this all the time, so it won't be obvious that I'm trying to set you up. That way you can see who you click with best."

Nicole's mouth curved into a tentative smile as she considered her friend's suggestion. She preferred meeting the guys first and deciding who she was more drawn to, if either. Her only concern was that there wouldn't be any expectation that she *had* to choose one.

"I like the party-"

"Great!" Kiko exclaimed. "I'll tell Dom and we'll send out the invites tomorrow."

"But," Nicole fixed her with a petulant glare, "I reserve the right to refuse them both."

"Ok," Kiko answered, a bit deflated. She wanted to do this for her friend but didn't want to waste her time. "But you have to seriously consider them and not just show up to the party and brood."

"I promise." Nicole said with a hand over her heart and a solemn expression.

Kiko shot her a withering glance before reaching for her glass. "In that case. Let's toast to you being face down, ass up before Thanksgiving."

Grinning, Nicole lifted her glass. "Let's shoot for Halloween."

"Ok! Get you a lil birthday sex," Kiko sang. "Speaking of which, we gotta plan something for your special day?"

"Can you swing two parties in one month?"

"Girl," Kiko purred. "Watch me work!"

∞ ∞ ∞

True to her word, Kiko pulled the mixer together in less than a week, with a decent number of RSVPs. She explained to Nicole that she invited a few of her other single girlfriends and Dom's friends to make it more interesting. She was sure Nicole would pick one of her two options, but didn't want to make it seem like a dating show.

Getting dressed for the party was an event in itself. Kiko drove over to Nicole's when collaborating over Facetime started to stress her out.

"This is so hard because you look bomb in everything, but let's eliminate some of these options."

She regarded each outfit splayed across Nicole's bed, forehead puckered, and lips drawn in a straight line. The stylist in her was working overtime as she attempted to create a look that was sexy, so much so that a man couldn't think.

While Kiko was considering those choices, Nicole was still rifling through her closet. She knew the look she was going for, fun and flirty, which conflicted a bit with her friend's sexy stunner theme. There was a little black dress that she'd bought, but never worn, that would be perfect. When she found it, her eyes lit up and she immediately tried it on, walking into the bedroom like she was on a runway.

"So, I'm thinking the red-" Kiko lost her train of thought when she saw her friend saunter past her.

"You like?" Nicole modeled the dress in her full-length mirror as she waited for a response.

"I love," Kiko drawled. "If you had shown me this before, I could have stayed my ass at home. It's just short enough, just tight enough, and shows just enough of your luscious tatas."

"Right?" Nicole beamed as she felt excitement begin to simmer in her tummy. She hadn't dressed up for a date or anything close in a long time. It felt good, and the prospect of being able to flirt and be girly made her smile grow wider.

Kiko smiled on like a proud mama. "Look at you, feeling yourself!"

"I am." Nicole did a little dance, shaking her butt and pumping her fists.

"Good. Now I'm gonna go home and finish getting everything together."

Kiko blew her a kiss as she grabbed her bag and dashed out. Nicole Facetimed Chelle to share in her excitement.

"Yo." Chelle appeared on the screen covered in a green face mask and Nicole grimaced and pulled the phone away.

"Fuck you," Chelle chuckled and stuck up the

middle finger. "You're the one who put me on to this damn mask. Now I do it once a week. Faithfully."

Nicole laughed. "It's damn good, though. Right?"

"Skin as smooth as a baby's," Chelle agreed. "Wassup."

Nicole walked over to her mirror, panning the phone the full length so that Chelle could see her dress. "I think this is perfect for the party."

"Nice," Chelle purred. "It's sexy without doing too much. Your body does enough on its own."

"I know that's right," Nicole giggled.

"I have a feeling this night is gonna be interesting. I'm so mad I'm not there. Next time y'all plan things like this in advance so I can attend."

"Sorry bookie. Time was of the essence. It had to be this weekend."

"I know. Don't mind me, I'm not hating or nothing." Chelle rolled her eyes.

"Stop that," Nicole laughed. "But I do feel like it's gonna be interesting too. I'm kinda getting butterflies in my belly."

"Is Jay gonna be there?" Chelle asked with a raised brow.

"Maybe," Nicole shrugged. "Probably. Why?"

"Well, you know life is about timing. Now you're single and he's single. So, we'll see what happens," Chelle mimicked Nicole's advice for her and Remy.

"Shut up, Chelle," Nicole griped.

"Wish I could see the look on his face when he

sees you in that dress," Chelle continued.

"Who cares? Remember, tonight is about me getting my groove back," Nicole stated.

"I know. Just my thoughts," Chelle quipped.

"Yeah, yeah," Nicole groaned. "Get off my phone."

"Whatever. You called me. Bye!"

Chelle's face disappeared as she hung up. Nicole laughed and tossed her phone on the bed. She wished her friend was there too, and the mention of Jay caused her to wonder what his reaction would be, and why it mattered.

Nicole finished getting ready for the party with more pep in her step than she'd had since her college days. She couldn't remember the last time she had been that excited to get dressed up and be seen. It was also the first time that she was going out to attract other men since she'd been in a relationship with the same man since her early teens. It was a foreign yet enchanting feeling.

The drive to Kiko's took no time. When Nicole pulled up to the gate she was buzzed through and drove up to the valet. Her phone dinged with a message, and she waited until she was out of the car to check to see who it was.

```
Kiko: Can you stop by Jay's?  I need
you to pick something up.
Nicole: Ok...
Kiko: The elevator code is 3576.
```

She stared at the message for a moment, wondering what he could possibly have that they needed for the party. Her mood shifted a bit, because not only was her carefully curated entrance ruined, but she also had to go to Jay's apartment, which she vowed never to do.

Stepping off the elevator to his floor, she was struck with a case of nerves. It irked her to no end that the thought of seeing Jay had her reacting in any way. She wished that she could be neutral toward him like she was toward their friend Shane, whom she loved like a cousin. No, it was different with Jay. Even when he was annoying her, it was because he managed to get under her skin.

The soft hum of music coming from his apartment made her hesitate before knocking. She put her ear to the door and heard the bright horns of a jazz ensemble. Her brows quirked as yet another facet of this man's nature threw her for a loop. Pressing the button for his bell, she stood there listening to the soothing melodic tune, zoning out as she became lost in the music.

When the door opened, she came face to face with a bare, sculpted chest with beads of water etching trails southbound over his taut abs and disappearing into the towel he clutched at his waist. Was she staring at a dick print? Coming to her senses, Nicole looked up to find Jay assessing her with a roguish smile while his eyes traveled down her body as he took her in from head to toe. The way his eyes lit up, she figured he liked what he saw.

"Damn, you look amazing."

"Thank you," she replied, and when he didn't move, she asked, "I'm here to pick something up, right?"

Jay stepped back and Nicole entered his space, feeling like she was walking into the lion's den. The music set the mood, but the ambiance was top tier. His apartment reminded her of a Manhattan speakeasy she'd been to once, with walls lined with top-of-the-line polished wood panels and gold fixtures. The lighting was dim, yet cozy, and his furniture was all neutral and earth tones. It reminded her of a luxury yacht cabin.

He closed the door behind her, placing a hand on her mid back to guide her further inside. That slight gesture stirred something deep inside that was begging for attention. Again, Nicole caught herself becoming lost in her thoughts and snapped out of it.

"I love how you've decorated your place. It's so..." She couldn't find the words as she continued to drink in the details. "Warm and inviting."

"You seem surprised," he said as he padded past her toward his bar.

"A little," she admitted. "I figured you for a more

modern look."

Jay looked around his place and shrugged. "That's funny because at first, that's the look I envisioned, but when I started getting into the process and pulling pieces, I wanted something different. Something deeper."

Nicole fingered an old-fashioned gold-plated clock perched on an antique console against a slate accent wall. She could tell he put a lot of time and effort into creating his space. The music captured her attention again; sultry vocals from a woman who sang about her lover saving his love for her.

"Who's singing? I love her voice. The way she enunciates each word so crisply."

"Ah, that's Nancy Wilson. Jackson put me on to jazz when he coached us at FAM. Used to play it to help me focus on my free throws. Said hip hop was a good motivational tool but jazz is more soothing so you can relax and really connect with what you're doing."

Nodding, Nicole understood the reference because she'd felt the effect after a few short moments. Jay observed her as she hummed the tune, clearly feeling it.

"Now I'm surprised. Nicole the hip-hop princess likes romantic jazz."

Nicole smirked. "Aren't you supposed to be giving me something?"

"Hmph." Jay's eyes glimmered with naughtiness, but he didn't say another word.

 Opening a cabinet above his head he removed a bag from a wooden box and placed it into a similar box but smaller. Not looking at him was almost impossible with his damn near next to naked body stretching and flexing. The towel did little to hide his shape, which was a work of art. He wasn't bodybuilder muscular, but all his muscles were nicely defined. Nicole swallowed hard, blaming her dry spell for why she was ogling her friend.

Jay seemed to be unaware of her over awareness of him with the ease he maneuvered around as if he were totally dressed. Grabbing his cell phone, he placed a call, verifying an amount of something with the person on the other line. Once he received the number, he hung up and took the box and placed it into a paper shopping bag and turned back toward Nicole. The scent of weed wafted through the air, and she understood her assignment.

"Here you go." He handed her the bag, letting his fingers slip over hers, and taking another opportunity to check her out. "That dress is..." There was a pause as he looked her over again, this time his eyes lingering on her heels before sliding up toward her thighs, then her cleavage, and finally her eyes. "Stunning. You are stunning."

Nicole found her throat to be suddenly dry and felt like the temperature in the room had gone up. A feeling of warmth spread throughout her body, starting from her center. "Thank you," she managed. She pulled her fingers from his hand and turned toward the door, highly aware that his eyes were on her, so she put a little umph in the sway of her hips.

"Shit," he gritted through his teeth at the way her curves were accentuated by that dress. "Maybe I need to come to this party."
"Maybe," she murmured over her shoulder as she opened the door. Turning to twiddle her fingers at him as she walked out. Jay trotted after her, catching the door before it shut. Leaning against the door jamb, he watched as she sashayed down the hall back toward the elevator.

"Damn," he groaned under his breath.

Chapter 5

Inside the elevator, Nicole crumpled against the wall. She felt like if she had stayed a moment longer, she would never leave. What was wrong with her? Gulping down deep breaths to calm herself, she thought of who she could call to discuss what just happened.

She was about to call Chelle but paused because she didn't feel like hearing jokes about them being together, so she called Joey instead. She made up the fourth peg in their friend group, but she was moving and shaking out in Los Angeles, so they didn't see her much. Her carefree spirit was just what Nicole needed.

"Hey boo!" Joey's bubbly personality emanated through the phone.
"Hey girl," Nicole huffed, still hot and bothered.
"Busy?"
There was a bit of shuffling and then Joey said, "I'm free. What's wrong? Why do you sound like

you've been running?"

"Girl, I don't know. I just left Jay's apartment and I'm trippin'."

Joey giggled. "Girl, why?"

"He was wet. Only wearing a damn towel."

"Mmmm," Joey purred. "Tell me more."

"There was jazz music playing and his apartment was such a mood. So sexy," Nicole uttered as she visualized it in her mind.

"His *apartment* was sexy, huh? So, what happened?" Joey could barely mask her amusement at Nicole's dramatic depiction of events.

"Nothing happened! I ran up outta there."

Joey's laughter tumbled through the speaker as she finally gave in to her thoughts. "That's that player vibe for you."

"Right? I felt like it was a friggin' trap," Nicole barked out in a hushed tone. She was walking through the lobby toward Kiko's elevator bank and was careful so that any potential party goer didn't overhear her conversation.

"Oh, it was definitely a trap," Joey agreed. "Straight out of the player handbook. He came to the door in a towel? Jay is ruthless!" She continued to giggle.

"What's so damn funny?" Nicole felt like there was an inside joke that she was missing.

"Because! Jay's probably been dying to do that to you."

Nicole wrinkled her nose. "So, he tried to do me like all the other chicks he's been with?"

"No, not like any other chick. C'mon Nicole. You know Jay's had a crush on you for years," Joey replied.

"Who hasn't he had a crush on?" Nicole was wary that this call was going in the direction she'd been trying to avoid.

"I don't know of anybody else he's ever had a crush on. Maybe girls he wanted to smash, but not anyone that he truly liked."

"Joey," Nicole deadpanned. "Are you serious? I don't have time for this."

"Hey. Don't shoot the messenger."

"Whatever. When are you coming down here?" Nicole switched gears, not wanting to have another conversation about her getting with Jay.

"I'll be there for your birthday, babe," Joey answered.

"Ok. Can't wait to see you." Nicole glanced up at the floor counter to see where the elevator was.

"Can't wait to see you guys too. Love ya!"

Joey ended the call, and Nicole slipped her phone back into her purse. She let out a deep breath as she tried to clear her mind. Jay was an attractive guy, and he was half naked. Her reaction to him would have happened with any good-looking guy in that scenario, she reasoned with herself. It would be nice if she had a friend she could have girl talk about the situation and it not turn into an episode of a The Love Connection.

A signal dinged and the elevator doors slid open.

Nicole stepped in, turning her back to the wall and pressed P to take her to Kiko's penthouse, then entered the code she had used when she stayed with them. Just as the doors were closing, she heard heels clicking against the buffed granite tiles, and a voice call out. "Hold the door!"

Nicole slipped her bag between the doors to keep them from shutting on the other woman.

"Thank you," the stranger gushed as she straightened her dress. It was a different variation of a little black dress, and the woman had hers paired with hot pink stilettos and a wristlet. She looked like a black Barbie doll.

"Nice dress," Nicole complimented.
"Aww, thank you. You look hot as hell, too. Are you going to Kiko's?"
"Actually, I am," Nicole admitted. She was almost tempted to say that the party was in her honor, but she held it in.
"Cool. I'm Mallory."
"I'm Nicole. I went to college with Kiko."
"Oh! Nicole. You just moved down here from New York," Mallory said excitedly.
"Yeah. That's me."
"My cousin plays with Dom, so I met Kiko a couple of years ago. This is so cool. I've been looking forward to meeting you. She said we would hit it off."
Nicole smiled. "Cool. I was hoping to make new

friends. You should come to brunch with us tomorrow."

The elevator came to a stop and the doors opened. Nicole motioned for Mallory to exit first, so that she wouldn't be the first to enter the party. Music was already pumping from Kiko's door, and the buzz of multiple voices reverberated in the hall.

"I think we're fashionably late," Mallory noted. "Perfect." Nicole winked and they strutted into the party.

There were already about twenty people scattered throughout Kiko's sprawling living room. Some of the furniture had been removed and replaced with high top tables and bar stools. There was a bar and bartender making drinks for a few of the guests, which was a nice mixture of Dom's teammates and single ladies.

Walking into the party, Nicole wasn't nervous at all. The encounter with Jay seemed to cover her in some sort of warm and fuzzy haze and she found herself gliding along. It was like an ice breaker before the main event. She bobbed her head to "Hood Nigga" by Gorilla Zoe as her eyes surveyed the room, looking for Kiko.

"Well, this looks promising," Mallory drawled, tucking her chin length bob behind her ears. "I'd say so," Nicole agreed. They exchanged a mischievous glance and continued their way through the room. "Let's get a drink," she suggested, wanting something to do so she could anchor herself.

They were off to the side of the bar, sipping their drinks when Kiko came swirling into the room. Dressed in a sexy gold jumpsuit, her weave hung to her midback in a pin-straight style with a deep side part. She was in full hostess mode and made her rounds to say hello to everyone and encouraged them to partake of the bar and the Hors D'oeuvres. When she saw Nicole, she rushed over.

"Hi baby!" As usual, she attacked Nicole with hugs and kisses. "And you two found each other." She turned to give Mallory her signature two cheek air kiss.

"Yes. I'm already crashing your brunch tomorrow," Mallory said.
"Fantastic," Kiko gushed. "I knew you two would click."
"You did say that," Mallory chirped.
"So, what do you think of the party?" Kiko's question was aimed at Nicole, but both her and Mallory nodded their heads in approval.
"I'm ready to mingle," Nicole said.
"I see a few prospects, Mallory said.

Just then, Kiko was approached by one of the guys, and Nicole recognized him from the pictures. It was Vance. He spoke with Kiko, but his eyes kept flitting to Nicole. She flashed him a demure smile and then turned her attention to Mallory, who was asking her a question.

"So do you know anyone here?"
"Is that your way of asking if I've dated any of the guys?" Nicole gave her a knowing look and Mallory grinned.
"Listen, I don't want to step on any toes. We just met, and I'd hate for it to come to an end over some man."
Nicole laughed. "No, you're right. And no, I haven't dated anyone here, even though I do have my eye on a couple of guys."
"Ok. Tell me who, so I can steer clear. I've hung out with the team but haven't dated any of the guys either. My brother won't introduce me to anyone, so I figured this is my chance to meet them on my own."
"Ladies," Kiko interrupted. "This is Vance. Vance, this is Mallory, and my friend Nicole. She just moved down from New York."
"Nice to meet you ladies," he said, but his handshake with Nicole lingered.
"Kiko," Mallory said, pulling her arm into hers. "Let's go harass Dom." She winked at Nicole as she led Kiko away.
"That wasn't obvious at all," Nicole chuckled.
Vance laughed. "It was, a little. That's cool though. Gives me the opportunity to have you to

myself, for a bit. I see the sharks circling already."

"You do?" Nicole took a quick glance around and saw a few eyes on them. One pair being De-Shawn, the other guy Kiko had shown her a picture of. He raised his drink to her, making no secret that he was watching her. "Wow, I hadn't noticed before you mentioned it.

"That's why I came over. I wasn't going to sit back and wait for someone else to tie you up."

"Smart move."

"So, how are you liking Miami?"

"I love it so far," she smiled. "The weather is gorgeous, and the blend of cultures is similar to New York. I'm still getting a feel for things, though."

"Well, I'd love to show you around. Take you to a few of my favorite spots."

The cockiness that she had detected in the pictures was there, but just slightly. Vance, so far, came across as a confident, straightforward guy. While he was attractive, he wasn't behaving like she was supposed to be throwing her panties like some guys do, and she found that to be a turn on. If anything, he just seemed to have a serious personality which was refreshing.

"Thanks for the offer, Vance. I was just telling Kiko I'm ready to mingle and make some new friends.

He perked up a bit and flashed her a mouth full of perfect teeth. "Excellent. I'll get your number from Kiko. Don't need to have everyone up in your business."

"Smooth," Nicole grinned.

"Hey. I'm just being considerate. Give me your phone and I'll put my number in there right now."

What would Joey do? Nicole knew he had a point. The entire room didn't need to know they exchanged numbers. Or did it even matter?

"You can give me yours." She pulled her cell phone out of her bag and tapped on the icon for her contacts. She typed in his name and said, "Ok. Shoot."

For anyone looking, she could have been doing anything on her phone and he could have been saying anything as he recited his digits to her.

"So, let's set something up for next Thursday if you're available. We have a home game, so I'll be in town for the weekend."

"Sounds good to me." She smiled again. Liking the vibe between them, and the fact that he got straight to the point.

"I'm glad I came over to talk to you. It's been a pleasure, Ms. Nicole.

"Mr. Vance." She batted her lashes at him, and he grinned.

"I like the way you say *Mr. Vance*."

"Well, if you're lucky. You'll get to hear me call you that again."

Vance smiled and nodded. Giving her a smoldering glance as he backed away, and then turned to rejoin his boys. Nicole released a deep breath and took a sip of her drink. Vance was hot. It was understated, but he had something intriguing about him. She turned her attention back to the party.

The crowd had grown a bit more and she assessed the newcomers. The person walking through the door caught her eye, and his gaze landed on her at the same moment. He smiled at her. Making his way through the crowd, stopping to say hi to a few of the guys.

Jay was dressed casually, for him, in a long sleeve white button down with the top few buttons open to reveal a peak at his chest, which she remembered vividly, and a pair of dark denim jeans. His olive-green suede ankle boots elevated the simple look to another level. He was always polished and put together.

Mallory rejoined Nicole, handing her another drink as they observed the crowd together.

"So how did things go with Vance?" She gave Nicole a hopeful smile.

"It was cute. I got his number, so we'll see how this goes," Nicole replied.

"Nice," Mallory said, but Nicole wasn't paying attention, so she followed the direction of where she was looking and saw Jay headed toward them.

"Is Jay the other guy that was on your radar? He. Is. Fine." Mallory checked him out from head to toe as he walked up to Nicole.

"Hey, you. Watchu sippin' on?" He took her drink out of her hand and took a sip before she could even object.

"Um! Excuse me," she protested, trying not to make a scene as she took her glass back. "Sometimes you act like you have no damn home training."

"I just wanted to taste your drink. What's the big deal?"

Mallory cleared her throat and Nicole gave her an apologetic look.

"Jay, this is Mallory, Kiko's friend. Mallory, this is Jay. We went to college together."

Jay took her hand in his and kissed it. Nicole got to see his player ways up close as he turned on the charm. "Pleasure to meet you," he said smoothly.

Mallory blushed and preened under his smile. "Nice to meet you, too."

"Now why haven't I met you before?" He tilted his head and hit her with a lopsided grin that had her blushing from ear to ear. Nicole tried to suppress her amusement, but a tiny part of her didn't want to watch any more of his show. She fixed him with her fakest smile and asked,

"Don't you have somewhere to be? People to see?"

"Am I cramping your style? I heard you were back on the prowl," he teased.

"If I had something besides this little purse, I'd hit you with it," Nicole threatened.

Jay laughed. "Fine. I'll leave you alone. Mallory, I hope to see more of you, soon."

Mallory all but gaped at him as he left on that double entendre. Nicole shot daggers at his back as he walked over to the bar and struck up a conversation with two women who were standing there. The way one threw her head back and cackled, she assumed they were drinking Jay's kool-aide.

"So, is he one of your guys or not? Cause I don't know if I should be turned on or confused."

"He is not one of my guys," Nicole clarified. She turned her back on Jay so that he wouldn't be in her line of sight and caught Mallory giving her a skeptical glare.

"He's not?"

Nicole laughed. "No, he's not. I told you. He went to school with me and Kiko. Jay's just a big flirt."

"Hmmm." Mallory looked over Nicole's shoulder and then back at her face. "Are you sure? He may be a flirt, but he seemed to be really into you."

"Not you too," Nicole groaned.

"I'm assuming you've heard this before?" Mallory chuckled. "I knew I wasn't bugging. So, he's off limits. Check."

"Could we not?" Nicole was done discussing Jay. "I'm ready to mingle a bit. Should we split up or make the rounds together?"

Mallory regarded her slyly before saying, "I think we should do it together. Put some pressure on these mofos."

"Mallory? Where are you from?"

"Yonkers," she replied with a grin.

"I'm from Queens. I knew I heard that accent."

"See." Mallory linked her arms with Nicole." We were meant to be!"

The duo spent the rest of the night networking and cutting up with Kiko. Nicole met a few guys, got a couple more numbers, and even met De-Shawn. He was nice, but mostly stared at her smiling while she tried to strike up a conversation. She was glad for the party because that date would have been like pulling teeth. Mallory seemed to hit it off with a guy who introduced himself as an entrepreneur.

Nicole really let her hair down, dancing and chatting with new people all night. Kiko introduced her to the other single ladies, and they planned a girl's night out. She flirted with every guy, even if she wasn't interested. A tip she learned from Joey.

All in all, the night was a success. She secured a date with Vance and had a couple of other guys on her radar. Kiko was ecstatic and discussed the possibility of throwing a singles mixer at a larger venue as a once-a-month event. Everyone thought that was a great idea. Jay stayed out of Nicole's hair, but she could feel his eyes on her all night. She pretended not to notice but couldn't ignore the tingles.

The party was over, and Kiko was directing the clean-up crew on where to put things, and Dom and a couple of guys were on the balcony smoking cigars.

"This was so much fun," Nicole exhaled as she plopped on Kiko's couch. She hiccupped and then giggled. "I think I need some water."

Jay came and lounged on the couch next to her, spreading his long arms across the back where she rested her head, which she lifted to make room for him. "You look like you enjoyed yourself."

Nicole leaned her head back against his arm. "I haven't had this much fun in years."

"Get any numbers tonight?"

She looked at him and blinked. "Why do you ask?"

"I want to know who it is. Make sure he's legit," he

explained.

"You say that like I only got one number," she joked.

"Ok, then I'll rephrase. Tell me who gave you their number so that I can approve them."

"Approve deez nuts," she cackled and then ambled to her feet.

"I'm serious." His humorless expression caused her to laugh even more.

"Jay, please. I can take care of myself," she snorted. "Kiko! I'm out," she called over the scraping sounds of furniture being moved.

"Call me when you get home," Kiko yelled back.

"I'll walk you to your car," Jay offered.

"I valet parked."

"Then I'll stand with you until your car pulls up to the curb." He strode ahead of her to the door and held it open as she walked through it.

"I really don't need you to babysit me," she grumbled as they waited for the elevator.

Jay smirked but he remained silent as he leaned up against the wall and took her in. Nicole shrugged, turning her head away. When the doors opened, she stepped in and moved all the way to the left. He stood to the right, back against the wall, and resumed his appraisal of her. Nicole wanted so badly to ask him why he was staring at her, but part of her wanted to see where he was going to go with it all. So, she continued to pretend he wasn't there, shifting from one foot to the other because her feet had given up on her five-inch heels.

When they reached the lobby, Nicole waddled ahead, and Jay strolled behind her. He let her take a few steps and then swept her up in his arms.

"Jay!" She struggled for a bit, but knew it was useless. "What are you doing?"
"Your feet hurt," he simply stated.
"I was fine," she argued.
"You were limping. I couldn't let you go out like that. Not in that dress."
"You're so ridiculous," she complained, but she was laughing the whole time.
"No, you looked ridiculous; moving like a crab."
"Shut up, Jay," she chortled.
He veered toward his elevator bank, and she began to struggle again. "What are you doing? Jay, take me to the valet. Now!"

This time he laughed at her panicked response and turned back toward the lobby doors. When they reached the valet stand, he put her down gingerly and she handed the attendant her ticket. He knelt in front of her, and Nicole felt a heat rising up her neck as he undid the straps on her heels and pulled her feet out one by one. Then he picked her up again.

"Ok, now you're just dragging it," she said.
"Doesn't that feel so much better?"
"It kinda does," she grinned.

"You're such a brat. Kinda?" He shook his head, watching as her car was parked in front of them. Stepping off the curb, he walked to the driver's side. This time he released her so that her body slid against his until her feet touched the ground. Nicole's breath hitched at the feel of the hard planes of his body up close, and very personal. He was so close she could still feel the heat from his body piercing hers, or maybe she imagined it so.

"Are you good to drive?" His voice dropped to that low octave that made her weak in the knees. "I'm good," she replied with a smile. "Thank you for the ride, by the way."

 He lifted a brow and said, "That's not the kind of ride I picture in my mind."

"Behave! You know what I meant," She nudged his shoulder. "Thanks for carrying me."

"You're welcome." He stared into her eyes, and she was unable to look away from the hungry glimmer she saw there.

"Good night, Jay."

"Aren't you forgetting something?"

"Oh," she breathed. She slid her arms around his waist for a hug, but he had something more in mind. She peered up at him when he didn't hug her back, and he grasped her chin and gave her a gentle kiss on her cheek. Nicole's body shuddered against his as he held her captive with his mouth while he placed a few soft kisses on her cheeks and nose, and then brushed his lips against hers as she turned her head away.

"Still playing hard to get," he whispered against her cheek. Nicole quivered as his deep voice created a volcano between her legs.
"I'm not playing," she uttered even though they both knew it wasn't quite true.
"Neither am I, love," he said with his lips brushing hers. "Good night, Nicky."

Nicole stood there panting softly, her fingertips trailing where his mouth had just been, as he turned toward the building. She watched his seductively masculine frame swagger away and realized she had a problem.

"Damn," she murmured.

Chapter 6

"**I** can't believe you're drinking ginger ale," Kiko complained as Nicole passed on their usual champagne heavy mimosas at brunch the next day.

"Yeah, well, I drank a lot last night, and even though I wasn't drunk when I left, my stomach is surely feeling the effects. I just need some good food in my belly."

"You were throwing them back at one point," Mallory agreed. "I'll have the pancakes and a side of scrambled eggs," she told the waiter who had come to take their order.

"I'll have the sausage, egg, and cheese panini with a side of cheese grits," Nicole ordered.

"Mmm. That sounds good," Kiko replied as she contemplated her order. "I'll have the same thing."

They thanked the server and handed over their menus. Kiko topped up her glass with orange juice, and Mallory sipped on her rum punch. Their silence was comfortable as a cooling ocean breeze blew in from the Atlantic. The trendy South Beach eatery was teeming with tourists, locals enjoying the gorgeous weather, and other regular brunchers like them who came almost every weekend.

"So," Mallory dragged out as she placed her glass on the table and steepled her fingers. "What's the deal with Jay?"

Kiko raised her brow and glanced at Nicole, who despite her best efforts was blushing. She still wasn't sure if she had recovered from his almost kiss in the parking lot. Grabbing her drink and taking a sip to buy her some time to get her thoughts together, she avoided eye contact until she was ready to talk.

"No comment," she finally said.
"Nuh uh," Kiko sputtered. "You made us sit here waiting for an answer, so you better have something more than that to say.
"I'm just asking because you would have to be deaf, dumb, and blind not to notice the chemistry between yall. So, what's up?"

Nicole placed both hands to her cheeks and let out a low growl. The truth was, she didn't know what was going on between her and Jay.

"I really don't know what I'm supposed to say. Do I find him attractive? Ye-"
"Yes," Kiko blurted out before she could finish.
"Yes," Nicole echoed, glaring at her friend. "Does he find me attractive?"
"Hell yes," Mallory confirmed.
"And that's all I got for ya." Nicole shrugged.
"But Nick... You know he's into you," Kiko replied.
"That's very evident," Mallory chimed in.
"So?" Nicole couldn't understand why everyone insisted on selling the idea of him to her.
"So? You're single and looking to," Kiko glanced around at the surrounding tables and lowered her voice a bit, "*adult fun*. Why not Jay?"
"Because," Nicole groaned. "I don't want to ruin our friendship if he wants more than that."
"And what if he does? Mallory asked. "What's wrong with that?"
"Because I'm not even officially divorced yet, and Trey was the only man I've ever been with. I want to know what it feels like to date and have fun without anything serious."
Mallory looked to Kiko for a rebuttal, but she just gave her the 'Girl, I don't know' face.
"That makes perfect sense, but I don't think you understand how treacherous dating is these days," Mallory stated.
"Right," Kiko agreed.
"And you might pass up on something that could

be good and real to dally with these 'un' mofos."

"What is 'un'?" Nicole asked using air quotes around un.

"Unreliable. Unavailable. Unbelievable. Undesirable. Unemployed. Un-"

"Ok," Nicole put a hand up for Mallory to stop. "I get it. I do. As it stands, I am going through a divorce. I have a date with Vance this week, so I'll see-"

"You know what I think?" Kiko cut her off, again. "I think you're afraid that *you* will be the one to catch feelings for Jay."

Nicole narrowed her eyes and poked out her lips. She let out a heavy sigh before saying, "Can we call an end to this little symposium on my love life, that I didn't ask for? Our breakfast is coming to the table, and I would like to enjoy my food, the tropical vibes, and maybe even a drink if this sandwich does me right."

The two other ladies looked at each other and shrugged. She was right, it was her love life and neither wanted to ruin brunch by pushing the subject.

"You got it, Boo," Kiko declared.

Later that evening, Nicole found herself pondering Kiko's assessment. The truth was that she'd just recently accepted her attraction to Jay and didn't quite understand if what she was feeling was anything worth exploring. The fact that she didn't have any experience was what really bothered her, and the fact that he had tons of experience made things worse. Sure, him being a player and getting hurt had crossed her mind, but more than anything, she wanted to learn more about who she was without being attached to a man.

Her cell phone went off and she reached over and plucked it off the bedside table, seeing Chelle's name glowing on the screen.

"Hey you," she said in greeting.

"Hey you right back," Chelle replied. "What's good? How was the party?"

"Chelle? I haven't had fun like that in a while." Nicole smiled as she recalled the events of the previous evening.

"That's good! Tell me everything," Chelle said excitedly.

So, Nicole launched into a play-by-play account of everything that happened. She entailed her tete-a tete at Jay's apartment, meeting Mallory in the elevator and hanging with her all night, talking to Vance and setting up a date, all the drinking and dancing, and ending with Jay carrying her because her feet hurt. For all her curiosity, Chelle didn't interrupt, riveted by certain parts of the story. Mainly, the parts with Jay.

"Damn, girl! That was one hell of a night," Chelle

finally said when Nicole came up for air.

"It really was. My feet were looking for a new owner by the time I was ready to leave," Nicole joked.

Chelle chuckled. "And Jay picked you up and carried you to the valet, took off your shoes and picked you up again?"

"Yeah," Nicole replied sheepishly. She was contemplating telling Chelle about their intimate moment and decided to when she realized she needed advice.

"Yeah," Chelle mimicked her. "And?"

"And," Nicole sighed. "And then he let me down very slowly so that my body slid down the length of his body, and I felt all his muscles."

"*All* his muscles?" Chelle asked.

"*Yes.* And then he said I was forgetting something, so I gave him a hug like last time but that wasn't what he meant."

"Last time?"

"Yeah, after he moved in my stuff. Anyways, that's another story. Then he grabbed my chin and placed these sweet little kisses on my cheek, and he just grazed my lips but then he pulled away and said good night."

There was silence after Nicole finished her story. She knew that Chelle would need to process what she'd said, but when it went on longer than she anticipated she got nervous.

"Hello?"

"Yeah, I'm still here," Chelle replied.

"Then why are you so quiet?" Nicole was on pins and needles for her response.

"I'm just sorting through everything you said and didn't say," she replied.

"Well while you're sorting, I have a question," Nicole said.

"Hit me." Chelle knew that it wasn't easy for Nicole to open up, so she refrained from the jokes and tried to focus on being supportive.

"What do you really think about Jay? Is he just toying with me, or do you think he's for real? Kiko thinks that if I'm gonna let anyone help me get my groove back, it should be him, but I don't want anything serious right now."

"That's a good question and an even better statement," Chelle replied. "I love Jay. Even more so since I've been with Remy. What I'm learning about him is that he does have that playful laid-back demeanor, but he can also be very deep."

"Hmm, ok," Nicole replied.

"He can be serious and goes after what he wants in a calculated way," Chelle continued. "I think he's had feelings for you for a long time, and now that there's nothing stopping him from flirting with you, he will. But I think he wants more than that."

"So, you think I should give him a chance, too," Nicole sighed.

"No, that's not what I'm saying. My question is how does his flirting make you feel? Because I noticed you haven't sucked your teeth or said, 'oh please' this entire conversation."

"I mean, he's sexy as hell, Chelle. Of course I'm feeling things, and I like it."

Chelle chuckled. "I bet you do like it. I think you should just be honest with him. He knows what you're going through with Trey and as a friend he's gonna be protective of you. Let him know that you just want to date, and that you're gonna date other people and see how things play out."

"Yeah," Nicole muttered. She thought about her pending date and possibly going out with some of the other guys she met, and even the prospect of meeting new people. "I have my date with Vance Thursday night, so I'm looking forward to that."

"This is gonna be your first adult date. Are you ready?"

"As ready as I'll ever be!"

Talking with Chelle left Nicole feeling lighter, and she felt like she had a better perspective on things. There wasn't any reason she couldn't enjoy flirting with Jay and explore her other options. She felt like maybe she was putting too much pressure on herself. It was time to focus on fun. Besides, it's not like it had *never* crossed her mind.

Kiko And Dom's Wedding - 2009

"Where do you think they're headed off to?" Nicole smirked as the table watched Chelle and Remy stroll out the back door of the banquet room that led to the beach. Joey, Jay, and Shane, all grinned, knowing they probably wouldn't be seeing the couple for the rest of the night.

"I bet they're just going to look at the stars," Joey said playfully.
"I bet he's about to make her see stars," Jay joked, and they all laughed.
"It's good to see them together. Warms my heart," Shane added.

The party was winding down, but the DJ was booked for another two hours, and a few people were still getting it in on the dance floor. None of the friends were ready for the night to end, so they sat together drinking and reminiscing. "Shawty is the Shit" by Dream came on and Joey jumped up.

"This is my *song*," she cried out as she began to rock her hips to the beat.

Soon enough Shane was on his feet, and they joined another group of people from college that were turning up to one of the songs that marked their senior year. Nicole and Jay both watched them and shook their heads. When they caught on that they held the same expression, they both laughed.

"So, what do you think about them?" Nicole nodded as Shane glared at Dante, Joey's latest boyfriend, who stepped in to dance with her.

Jay laughed at Shane's expression. "I just mind my business," he chuckled.

"Right," Nicole said, rolling her eyes.

"Well, what about you?" He asked her.

"What about me?"

"I've been asking, but I'll ask one *mo* time. Where ya man at?"

Nicole cut her eyes and released a long sigh. "No comment."

"Naw, fuck that." Jay leaned forward, not wanting to shout her business to the world. "What good reason could he have to not show up to this?"

"Well –"

"Man, whatever. Ain't none," he cut her off. "There's no way I'm letting my wife travel to a wedding on nobody's tropical island for a week by herself. *Especially* not looking like you do.

"Jay, please. You know how it is."

"No, Nicole. I don't know how it is. All I do know is that I've been watching that mufuka mishandle yo ass for too long."

"You're drunk," she grumbled. "And it's nothing

you need to worry about."

"I ain't that drunk," he defended. "And you're my friend, and I care about you. Of course it's my business."

"Baby Boy" by Sean Paul featuring Beyonce came on and Nicole jumped up, ready to change the subject. "Come on and dance. You're killing my vibe," she called over her shoulder.

On the dance floor is where she really came alive. Nicole could dance from the day she could walk, let her mother tell the story, and it was her favorite form of expression. Her sassy, confident, and sultry personality always shone through the artful way she moved her body. Being part Jamaican, she had learned all the reggae dances and would teach the rest of the crew. Jay, still a little upset from their conversation, just glared at her from his seat until the way her hips vacillated made him forget. It was like he was hypnotized and couldn't help but join her.

Maybe it was their conversation, the fact that Trey hadn't shown up, the fact that they were drinking, or the natural chemistry that she always denied, but Nicole didn't balk when he placed his hands on her tempting hips and wound his hips behind her. They moved in sync to the rhythm, getting the attention of Joey who began to cheer them on. Everyone was surprised to see Nicole letting someone besides Trey dance with her.

After a few more songs, the crowd had thinned out visibly and the only friend besides them that remained was Shane, who was dancing with one of Kiko's cousins. The DJ was closing out the night with slow jams with a few couples stuck around to enjoy the laid-back tempo. It had been a long time since Nicole had enjoyed herself so much or had danced like that and she wasn't ready to quit.

Jay had a hand lightly pressed to the base of her back and the other slung around her shoulder as they rocked to "Sexy Love" by Ne-Yo. He looked down at her, deep in thought, with her head perched on his shoulder and a content smile on her face. It was a far change from the frown she'd been wearing for most of the trip. He was just glad that she finally relaxed enough to dance so comfortably with him. They fit together like they'd done this a thousand times before.

Their pace slowed even more when "Comforter" by Shai began to play. Nicole's logical mind told her she should step away, but something about the moment felt so right, and not at all like something she had no business doing. For all his drunkenness, Jay wasn't crossing any lines, and being a gentleman. His hands weren't anywhere they shouldn't be, and he wasn't saying the inappropriate shit she used to have to cuss him out for.

As if sensing her dilemma, Jay leaned down and asked, "You good?"

Nicole pulled back to look up at him. "I should probably head to my room," she said with a small smile.

"What's the rush? This is one of my favorite songs. Don't leave yet."

"One of your favorite songs is a slow jam?" She glared at him full of skepticism.

"Ok, this is one of my favorite slow jams," he corrected.

"That makes more sense," she grinned.

"Stay?" His warm brown eyes silently beseeched her, and she rested her head against his chest as they continued to sway together.

Nicole convinced herself that it was harmless, just two friends dancing, but they were making her feel some type of way. The words were reminiscent of the things he'd said to her over the years. About wanting to be there for her and being a friend to comfort her. It made her notice things she shouldn't, like how good he smelled, or how firm his chest muscles were, or how she loved that he was much taller than her. The way his fingers flexed against her back and the way that caused a warmth to swirl deep down inside. Before she knew it, her body was pressed against him and he held her close, resting his chin atop her head.

"Hey! Where is everyone?" Chelle asked, scaring Nicole back to reality.

"Oh," she gasped when she thought of what they must have looked like, but when she caught sight of Chelle's appearance she laughed.

"Why do you look like you were shipwrecked? Where's Remy?"

"Shut up," Chelle chuckled as she swiped at the sand on her dress. "He's in the bathroom. I just came back for my wristlet and a piece of cake. Are you coming to the bar? We'll be at the one adjacent to the beach."

"Yep. We're right behind you," Jay called after her as she scurried to the doorway where Remy was waving to them. Jay gave him the two-finger salute before turning to grab his jacket.

Turning back to Nicole, he watched as she gathered herself and said goodnight to Kiko's family members who were sitting in the back and drinking. He'd always thought she was beautiful, but there was something about the way she was wearing that bridesmaids dress that did something to him. She deserved so much more than how her husband treated her.

"Let's go!"

She flashed him a big smile, already back to pretending that they hadn't just shared a moment. Jay shook his head and followed her out the same door that Chelle and Remy had gone through toward the beach. They walked in silence for a while, with him following behind her until she looked back and saw him lagging behind.

"What's up slow poke?"

"Nada," he said as he sipped on one of the bottles of champagne he had snagged on the way out of the banquet hall. The plan was for bubbly to be flowing all night, and of course Kiko had ordered enough to not run out. He handed it to Nicole who took a quick swig, and then a longer one when she found she liked the smooth taste.

"If nothing is wrong, why are you so quiet? You always have something to say."

"I'm just thinking."

"About what?"

"I really meant what I said earlier. You may think it's the liquor talking, but it's not."

"Ok," she replied, not wanting to rehash the conversation.

"You deserve better, Nick," he continued.

"I know that!" She rounded on him, with her arms spread wide. "Don't you think I know that?"

Her voice cracked and Jay felt it in his heart. He stepped toward her, and she stepped back.

"Do you think I'm stupid? Shit, maybe I am dumb. I just witnessed the most beautiful wedding, and my husband couldn't even be bothered to show up for me. You don't think I know how fucked up that is?"

This time when Jay stepped forward, she didn't back away. He wrapped his arms around her in a bear hug as she cried against his chest. She quivered in his arms as her sadness and anger ran its course. When she quieted, he pulled back, wiping her tears with his thumb when she looked up at him. The expression in her eyes reminded him of a sad puppy in a cage, and he wanted so badly to free her. Before he even knew what he was doing, his mouth was on her.

Caught off guard, she didn't have a chance to react before his soft lips were pressed to hers. In a feeble attempt to protest, she turned her head to the side, but his mouth chased hers.

"Jay, no," she whispered, even though her arms didn't let him go.
"Nicole," he breathed. She was everything. All that he could see, smell, or feel.

Having had a small taste of her, he needed more. He continued to place soft kisses across her face, while pleading for her lips again. Nicole trembled with the urge to kiss him back, but she was warring with her conscience, then remembered why she was even there alone in the first place, and she grabbed the sides of his face and placed her lips against his.

Thrusting his fingers through her hair, he cradled her head while his tongue devoured her mouth. Jay didn't know how long the kiss would last, or he'd be able to hold and caress her supple body, so he didn't waste a moment. The feel of her pouty lips and the taste of champagne were a heady combination. The sounds of her moans as she ran her hands up his back almost drove him wild.

Voices in the distance snapped Nicole back to reality, and she pulled back while pushing Jay away from her.

"I can't," she panted as she tried to catch her breath. She turned to go, looking panicked, but he caught hold of her wrist. He didn't know what he wanted to say, but he didn't want her to leave. Not like that.

"Jay, please," she said, still facing away from him, feeling embarrassed.

"Hey." He reached over, placing his fingertip to her chin to tilt her face toward him. They looked into each other's eyes and the warmth she saw in his allowed her to relax. She didn't fight it when he pulled her back into his arms for another hug. She inhaled his scent, committing it to memory, as if she knew she'd need the reminder. This time when she pulled away, he let her go.

Chapter 7

One of Nicole's favorite things about living in Florida, and there were a few, was shopping at Publix supermarket. She loved the size, cleanliness, and variety of food offerings. A typical visit included a trip to the deli counter for a loaded turkey sandwich, and the bakery for some freshly baked donuts. She was munching on one of the sweet treats while being rung up by the cashier when a familiar face made her freeze in place.

Trey had wandered into the entrance of the store, glancing toward the bakery like he was searching for someone. Nicole's heart stopped, and she did a double take, holding her breath as she prayed he didn't look her way. Thinking quickly, she pulled her sunglasses down over her eyes, and hunched over so that the guy bagging items in the next line would block her from his view. When he began to stroll deeper into the store, away from her, she breathed a sigh of relief. Quickly, she paid for her groceries, grabbed her bags, and hustled out the exit.

On her way to her car, she reached around in her purse for her cell phone, pulled it out and called Jay, praying, again, that he would answer. Kiko was at an away game with Dom, and Mallory didn't know about her drama with her apparently insane soon to be ex-husband. She was so lost in her thoughts that she almost screamed when Jay answered the call.

"Hey, you," he said.

"Jay," Nicole whispered. "I just saw Trey!"

"What? Where?"

"I was at the Publix by my house. He just walked in."

"Where are you now?"

"I'm about to get in my car. Oh my God, I'm freaking out," she gasped. Her shock finally wearing off and fear setting in. She almost dropped her bags as her fingers fumbled around her purse for her keys, while shooting quick glances back toward the store's exit. Then she remembered they were in the inside zipper pocket.

"Are you sure? Did he see you?"

"No. He didn't even look my way. But I'm sure he saw my car in the parking lot. I haven't changed my plates yet. What the fuck, Jay? Why is he here?"

"Ok. Try to calm down. I'm driving, but I can be at your house in about ten minutes. Don't get out of your car until you see me. Ok?"

She gulped. "Ok. I'm pulling out now."

Casting one last look toward the store, she still didn't see Trey emerge, but her level of paranoia was bubbling up, and she felt like he knew exactly where she was and what her next move was. As she drove out the shopping center parking lot, she felt like there was a target on her back. She wondered what frame of mind he was in to just show up like this, and how long had he been following her. The more she thought about it, the more she realized he had probably been staking out her house.

Too scared to stop, she drove around her neighborhood, deciding to wait for Jay to let her know he had arrived before parking. Not knowing what Trey's agenda was, or how he was getting around made her even more anxious, and she hoped he didn't somehow spot her in her attempt to hide. Looking at the time, only two minutes had passed since she hung up with Jay. The music from her radio was too much, so she turned it off, but then the silence made her nervous. Her phone ringing caused her to jump out of her skin. When she checked, it was a call from Chelle.

"Hey! You ok?" Chelle asked, sounding as frantic as Nicole felt.

"No! Why the fuck is Trey in Florida? What does he want?"

"Girl... I wish I knew. Jay just called me. Please don't let him do anything crazy. He sounds a little disturbed."

"I just hope Trey doesn't do anything crazy, 'cause I know Jay won't hesitate to throw hands."

"Yeah. But I think Jay works with a little bit more than his hands. You know everyone in that crazy ass state has a firearm."

"Chelle, please. I'm already freaking the fuck out. Don't make it worse."

"Sorry, boo. You know I'm just keeping it real. I'm just shocked that Trey's there. He's spent so much time acting like he didn't give a fuck about you, now he wants to turn into a stalker?"

"Right? I mean he hinted at it, but in all the time I lived twenty minutes from him, he never showed up uninvited. And he tried to roll up on me in the damn supermarket!"

"Publix?" Chelle sounded like that was the major offense.

"Hold on, Chelle. Jay is calling." Nicole put that call on hold while she clicked over and answered Jay.

"Hey," she said.

"I'm pulling up to your house. Where are you?"

"I'm coming right now," she replied.

"Ok."

Nicole clicked back over to Chelle, feeling more relieved knowing Jay was at her house. She didn't dwell on the feeling that hearing his voice inspired in her chest.

"Hey. He's at my place now. I was driving around aimlessly until he got there."

"Aww! I'm sorry this is happening. Maybe Trey just wants to talk.

"Maybe."

 Nicole's response was uttered absentmindedly, her focus now on Jay who was standing in front of her garage with his strong biceps folded across his white t-shirt clad chest. His distressed jeans fit snugly against his long legs and thighs. The stern expression on his face softened a bit when he made eye contact with her. Seeing how good he looked reminded her of how dressed down she was, just running into the store after working out at the gym.

"Are you there yet? Hello?" Chelle's question snapped her out of her daze.

"Yeah. I just pulled up. I'll keep you posted on how things turn out."

"Ok, babe. Please, be careful. I love you!"

"Love you, too," Nicole sighed as she disconnected the call.

Jay approached her car, helping her with the bags

as he cautiously surveyed the immediate area. Nicole's hands were shaking like a leaf as she tried to open her front door, so Jay grabbed the key from her and did it himself. Once they were inside, he put a hand up to halt her from entering further into the house.

Nicole gasped when he pulled a gun out of a holster attached to the waist of his pants.

"What are you doing with that?" She whisper-screamed while pointing at his .45 caliber.

"Shh," he hushed her. "I'm gonna make sure we're here alone. If you hear anything strange, call Jackson."

"*Jackson?* Not 911?"

Jackson Davidson was an assistant coach when they attended FAMU, and was now a notable businessman in South Florida, hailing from the same hood as Jay, Dom, and Kiko. He was only five years older but had always mentored the crew like an uncle.

Jay glared at her, placing a finger over his lips, motioning for her to be quiet as he went to inspect her place for an unwelcome visitor. Nicole watched him with wide eyes as he stalked away, gun cocked, and she prayed that Trey wasn't stupid enough to have broken in. She ran her hand through her hair, stressed, and accidentally knocked her earring loose. Cursing, she bent over to pick it up, checking the other ear to make sure they weren't both missing.

When he returned, Jay found her looking like she was on the verge of a breakdown.

"Nicole," he called out to her.

"I'm ok, she huffed. Just trying to –"

Before she could finish her sentence, Jay slipped his hands under her arms bringing her to a full standing position.

"Breathe, Nicole!"

"What the–"

"Take deep, slow breaths," he ordered.

"What are you doing?" She wrangled herself out of his clutches, looking at him like he was crazy.

"Oh, you're good?"

"I'm fine! What in the world?"

Jay let her go and released a deep breath. "I thought you were having a damn panic attack."

Nicole waited for him to laugh, but when she realized he was serious she cracked up instead.

"It's not funny," Jay deadpanned.

"I'm sorry, but you should have seen your face."

"Well, you're the one that called me all crazy. Can't blame me for being cautious."

"Right."

"Anyways," he said looking around. "How do you want to deal with this? Has Trey called you or anything?"

Nicole's mood dropped back down as she wandered to the kitchen for a bottle of water. "No, he hasn't called, and I'm not sure what to do. Should I call him?"

Jay contemplated her question for a minute, accepting the bottle she offered him then perched on a stool at her kitchen island. "Yeah. Maybe you should call him. See what he says, where his mind is at."

"Yeah," Nicole uttered. Dread filling her at the thought of what Trey had in mind. She took a deep breath as she scrolled through her phone to find Trey's blocked contact info, hesitating for a moment before placing the call.

"So yo ass did see me earlier," his voice boomed through the phone speaker.

"Trey? What are you doing?"

"I thought I might surprise you. There's no law against a man seeing his wife. Right?"

"Why would you show up in Florida unannounced? How did you know where to find me?"

As she spoke, the absurdity of what he'd done really hit her.

"It wasn't hard, really. But we can talk more when I get there."

"What? Don't come –" The call disconnected before she could finish telling him not to come.

"What did he say?" Jay saw the blood drain from her face as she stood there looking stunned.

"He's coming here. I don't want to deal with this," she cried. Pacing backing and forth with a hand to her forehead.

"Don't worry. I'll be here. I won't let anything happen to you."

"But I don't want anything to happen to you, either. I don't want anything to happen," she yelled, frazzled.

"Nicole," Jay's stern baritone crept through her paranoia, and she stilled. "I said, don't worry."

As if to punctuate his words, her doorbell rang, causing her to startle a bit. Jay placed a finger over his mouth to hush her.

"I'm gonna be right here. Open the door, but don't let him in. If he tries to force his way in, then I'll handle it."

Nicole nodded and headed toward her front door. Her stomach was doing summersaults, and her heart was clanging against her ribcage. She prayed, again, that Trey had acquired a modicum of sense since they last saw each other. The expression in Jay's eyes was serious and the last thing she wanted was for either of them to be hurt, much less herself.

When she opened the door, Trey was standing there with his arms folded across his chest. His long dreads had been neatly twisted away from his face, and his dark skin was glowing. She hated that such a promising specimen of a man had turned out to be such a waste, but she wasn't the first woman to pick a dud of a man, and she wouldn't be the last.

"So, this is what I gotta do to see you?"
"No, you could have done what normal people do and just ask. What do you want, Trey?"
"Can, I come inside?"

Nicole bit the inside of her cheek. She knew he would ask. "I don't think that's a good idea, considering the last time I saw you." She didn't bother to remind him of his aggressive behavior. "C'mon, Nick. I told you I'd never put my hands on you again."
"Well, you said that the previous incident and that didn't seem to mean much. Just say what you came to say. You know what I want from you, so I don't have anything else to say until I get it."
"I miss you. Shit! Acting like you slow. You took shit too far moving out of state without even telling me. How are we supposed to work shit out now?"
"We're not supposed to work shit out. That's the point," she said, getting agitated.
"I told you I want you back. I –"
"I want a fucking divorce," she yelled. "I'm not coming back. I don't want to be with you anymore. Stop playing these games. Sign the papers and move on!"
"You're the one playing games," he shouted, at-

tempting to push past her, but she shoved his chest.

"No. Go back to wherever you're staying. I'm done, Trey."

"Man, if you don't calm your ass down and let me in. I came all this way to –"

Again, his words were cut off, but this time it was the sight of Jay advancing on them that turned Trey's words to dust on his tongue. His eyes narrowed as he looked between the two and then a villainous laugh spilled across his lips.

"Oh, so this is why you're acting brand new. I don't think you want these kinds of problems, playboy," Trey said, revealing his own gun in the waistband of his jeans.

Jay simply laughed as he did the same. "I ain't worried," he replied, staring Trey down.

An evil grin slid across Trey's face as he reached for his piece, but before he was able to pull it all the way out, the appearance of three more men on Nicole's walkway halted him.

"I think you've overstayed your welcome, bruh," Jackson said, aiming his own .45 caliber at Trey's chest. He looked like the quintessential Florida thug, with a fitted black tee, camouflage pants, and a crisp pair of black Air Force One's. The two men flanking him, looking like south Florida's finest with gold grills gleaming and chunky free-form locs, sported similar outfits accessorized with semi-automatic rifles. "Why don't you step out here and let's have a friendly conversation."

"Wait here," Jay said.

Eyes wide, Nicole watched in shock as Trey glowered, nostrils flared, then took his hand off his gun. He gave Nicole one last long look, turned, and left. Jay stalked past her, following him down the path to where Jackson stood. She watched them have a heated discussion, straining her ears to hear what was said, but followed Jay's instructions to stay put. Before long, Trey walked off, getting into his car rental, and driving off. He never looked back.

Still feeling anxious, she closed her screen door and went and sat on her couch. She clenched her fists, then shook them out, trying to quell her nerves. A mixture of excitement and relief flowed through her veins as she processed what had just happened. Jay had called the damn cavalry out and ran Trey's gangsta ass off. A cackle bubbled up from her diaphragm and she slapped her hand over her mouth to keep from dissolving into a fit of hysterics.

Male voices approaching caught her attention and she stood up, eager to hear the details of what had transpired. When Jay walked inside, he did a quick scan and found her eyes. A moment transpired between them before a victorious smirk spread across his face. Ignoring him,

Nicole looked to Jackson.

"I can't believe you had my driveway looking like Bad Boys II," she joked.

"Jay told me you needed some reinforcements, so I brought a couple of friends. I told you we look out for each other in this group."

"Handled," Jay said, cocky as ever. Nicole couldn't even be mad at him if she wanted to.

"I've never seen Trey shut up so fast," she mused. "But I don't know how to feel about you showing up here with some goons."

"Look. We had to show him a lil Miami Dade hospitality. I doubt he'll be rolling up on you again, anytime soon," Jackson stated.

"Or, ever," Jay added.

"What did you say to him?" Nicole was curious to know what else drove Trey off.

"I just explained to him that you wasn't some average chick he could run down on like that," Jay replied.

"And I showed him the rest of our boys parked up and waiting, and that if he ever came back without your explicit invitation, I have some pet gators that I could serve him up to," Jackson added.

"Oh."

Nicole's eyes bugged out at the implication, and she realized this was the side of Jackson that people whispered about. Up until that night, she'd assumed the stories about him being deep in the streets as a teen and maintaining his connections through college and even after were rumors. The way Jay maneuvered the situation had her looking at him differently too. He caught her giving him the once over and their eyes locked, but her doorbell ringing broke their spell. The tingles creeping up her spine subsided as she looked away.

She took a step toward the door, but Jackson held his hand up to stall her progress.

"You don't think he would be dumb enough to come back?" She looked at him skeptically then to Jay who also looked on alert.

"He still calls you his wife. I know I'd burn this bitch down about my woman," Jackson declared as he turned to open the door. The serious expression on his face faded and a sly grin crept in before he unlocked the screen door to let Kiko in, "What the hell?" She eyed Jackson suspiciously, hesitating in shock, before returning the hug he was offering. "Chelle called me and said that Trey popped up. What are you guys doing? And why is there a gang meeting happening in front of your house?"

Kiko walked as she talked and was to Nicole in an instant, dramatically examining her for injuries. Nicole noticed that the entire time, Jackson had his eyes peeled on Kiko, who never gave him another glance. He must have realized he was staring, because he shook his head and snapped out of it.

"Trey did show up," Nicole confirmed. "But I thought you were out of town, that's why I didn't call you. Why aren't you with Dom?"

Kiko's jaw clenched slightly before she said, "Long story. Tell me about Trey."

Nicole's brows furrowed, but she didn't push the issue. Especially not with the guys present.

"I'm gonna head out," Jackson announced. "And break up the goon convention outside." He dapped up Jay, gave Nicole a salute, and nodded to Kiko as they exchanged some serious eye language.

"I'm gonna get out of here, too," Jay said as he headed to the kitchen to grab his keys and gun holster. Kiko gasped in surprise when she realized he was strapped.

"Damn, shit must have been serious," she said.

"Yeah, it got pretty intense," Nicole replied. "Jay and Jackson, along with the goon platoon, ran him out of town. I just hope he's not crazy enough to come back.

"Well, shit. You can't stay here tonight, at least not by yourself," Kiko said. "You want us to stay? Or you can come back to my place. We can have a movie night."

"Us?" Jay repeated. "I like how you volunteered me."

"I'm sure Jay has other plans," Nicole scoffed.

"Don't worry about it."

"I actually don't have plans," Jay replied.

"And I don't have a gun. So…" Kiko trailed off as she picked up on the tension between her friends.

"Then I guess I'm staying," Jay replied.

"Great. That's settled. What are we watching?" Kiko tossed her purse on the couch and pulled out her phone. "What do you guys want to eat?"

"I didn't agree to this," Nicole balked, but it was all talk. She was secretly relieved to not be alone. She just needed a few moments to herself to process but was grateful for the distraction.

"*Menace to Society*, *Love Jones*, *Boomerang*, or *Coming to America*?" Kiko listed their collective favorites.

"I lived out *Menace to Society* earlier, so I'll pass on that," Nicole sighed.

"How about *Boomerang*?" Jay offered.

"You suggest that every time, Jay," Nicole replied.

"How about *Love Jones*," Kiko squeaked.

"*Love Jones*?" Jay's voice held a wary tone.

"You don't like it?" Kiko asked, dumbfounded at the possibility.

"I've never seen the whole thing. The one time we all watched it, I fell asleep while he was talking about being a 'Brother to the night' or whatever."

Kiko laughed and Nicole shook her head, leaving them to work it out. She walked deeper into the house, choosing her bathroom as a place of refuge. Flipping on the light, she braced her palms on the counter as she stared at her reflection in the mirror. It felt like she was having an out of body experience and needed to reintegrate.

The image of Trey revealing his gun and then Jay flashing his kept playing over in her mind. What had Trey really intended to do? The possibilities made her shiver. It was still difficult to correlate the man she used to love with the man that he had become. The way that Jay had stepped up and taken care of things, no hesitation, really touched her.

A knock at the door caused her to flinch. Yep, her nerves were shot.
"You good, Nick?" Kiko's voice was filled with concern.
"Yeah," Nicole called back. "I'm just gonna take a quick shower. I was on my way home from the gym when this all popped off. I'll be out in a minute."
"Ok, boo." Kiko replied and then went to rejoin Jay.

Thirty minutes later, Nicole re-emerged in the living room, refreshed, in her PJs with a fresh set for Kiko to change into. Kiko was in the kitchen arranging the food she had ordered, and Jay was walking back inside with his gym bag. Once again, he made eye contact with Nicole and an unspoken sentiment transpired between them. He nodded, understanding that she appreciated him being there.

"Don't start the movie without me, I'm just gonna change real quick," he said as he headed for her guest bathroom.
"Keep a hoe bag in the trunk, huh?" Kiko teased. Jay smirked but didn't deny it.
"Stay ready, don't have to get ready," he replied.
"Right." Nicole rolled her eyes as she loaded up her plate with Pad Thai noodles.
"Whatever," Kiko giggled. "Just hurry up."

Once Jay was out of earshot, Kiko turned to Nicole.

"So, you really ok?"
"Honestly?" Nicole looked her in the eyes. "I don't know how to feel. I mean the way Jay and Jackson handled shit blew my mind. But then I think about what might have happened if they hadn't been here. What if I had been alone?"

Kiko put her plate down and gripped Nicole by the shoulders, giving her a long look.

"Listen, don't worry about what could have happened. Just know that we got you. Ok? Nothing did happen and you're safe and you can trust and believe that if Jackson says you're safe, then there's nothing to worry about."

Nicole nodded. Taking a deep breath as she tamped down an emotional outburst.

"I do feel relieved. It's just sad. That's all. I loved Trey. I still do in some way. I hate that it's come to this."

Kiko's eyes softened, and she gave Nicole a quick hug. "I understand that."

"Speaking of Jackson," Nicole said. "Am I buggin', or is there something up with that? What were the weird looks about?"

"Girl, nothing," Kiko said, biting the inside of her lip.

"Excuse me?" Nicole's tone said she wasn't letting that slide.

Kiko sighed. "I don't know. It just irks me that because he's known me since I was a kid, he thinks he can override me."

"Huh? Override you how?" Nicole wrinkled her brows in confusion.

"You know he discussed starting a business with Dom? Well, we've had a few differences of opinions." Kiko explained.

To Nicole, it sounded like there was more to the story, but for once she didn't push it. She'd do more digging when they had time to really talk about it.

"I hear you," she said, instead.

"Besides, the real story of the night is Jay," Kiko said, wiggling her brows.

"What about him?" Nicole snipped, but she couldn't hide the traces of a smile.

"Yeah. What about me?" Jay echoed as he re-joined them wearing a sleeveless t-shirt that showcased his sculpted physique, and a pair of gray sweats that had Nicole crossing her eyes trying not to stare at his bulge. When she looked up, he was giving her that knowing smirk that simultaneously irked and intrigued her.

"Shall we get started?" Nicole asked as she grabbed her plate and headed for the living room.

"I'm more than ready," Jay replied. His innuendo wasn't lost on Nicole, or Kiko who raised her brows in understanding.

Chapter 8

Time seemed to move at a breakneck speed for Nicole. She'd spent the majority of the week catching up on things for work and updating her personal website to her new location. Kiko referred her to a few of the other athlete wives who were interested in appearing in one of her articles, so her financial situation improved almost overnight. Their collaboration on the blog showcasing Kiko's work as a stylist was blowing up, and Jay helped them to find a store front that they could convert to an office/studio for their joint endeavors.

Despite whatever was brewing between them on the personal front, Jay proved to be an excellent partner on the business front. Nicole learned about his other projects during a networking event hosted by Jackson. Also known as JD, he held quarterly meetups to discuss possible group ventures and opportunities. It was his initial suggestion that the group find ways to elevate and make money together.

He was co-founder of a few joint ventures with the guys, including a recording studio he ran with Jay. Nicole soaked up all the knowledge that she could so that she could make some moves once her money was up. JD also helped Nicole and Kiko set up the organizational tax structure for their joint venture in the state of Florida. The vibes were still weird between them, but nothing Nicole could really question.

Whenever she wasn't devoting her time to work, she focused on making her house feel more like a home. After the incident with Trey, Jay insisted that she install an advanced security system that both he and Kiko would have access to. To his surprise, Nicole didn't even argue about it, agreeing that it was necessary. The days following the incident had been rough, especially being there alone.

She also ordered a few pieces of equipment that she would need in her home office, but planned to set up the room so that it could be a comfortable guest room for when she had visitors. Her mother was already chomping at the bit to come and see her, especially since New York had been experiencing a frigid fall. With each passing day, she fell more in love with her new circumstances.

Date night arrived in a flash. Vance, in an old-fashioned gesture, picked Nicole up from her house. Normally, she would have been against that, but she didn't really worry about it because if he did act up she knew where he worked and who his friends were. They chatted about their respective weeks as he made the short drive from her home to downtown Miami. He seemed even more handsome than when they met. She also wasn't mad at his manly, citrusy scent that hung in the air of his Porsche 911. Her hair fluttered in the light breeze as he whipped from lane to lane on i95 south, and Nicole enjoyed the new sensation of freedom.

He pointed out a few of his favorite spots before heading over the causeway that led to Zuma, a trendy Japanese restaurant that catered to a lot of celebrities. It didn't even cross Nicole's mind that being a pro athlete he would want to go somewhere flashy. She was glad that she had let Kiko style her for the date because she was dressed for the occasion. After handing the valet his keys, Vance grabbed her hand and led her to the hostess stand.

"Vance," the young woman squealed with the tinge of an eastern European accent. She looked to be all of twenty dressed in a short black blazer dress. Her platinum blond hair was slicked back into a severe ponytail, and her bright blue eyes were heavily lined with black liner. She beamed up at him as if he were there to change her life.

"Hey, Mila. I have a reservation for tonight," Vance said as he handed her five crisp hundred-dollar bills. Mila looked at Nicole for the first time, openly assessed her from head to toe and then, seeming to approve, smiled.

"Follow me. Your favorite table is ready." Mila mumbled something to the other hostess who had just walked up, grabbed two menus, and gestured for them to follow behind her. She led them to a table almost in the center of the restaurant and Nicole had to school her features as she wondered how often he frequented the place, and if he enjoyed being the center of attention that much. She thought about how she had initially passed on his picture, sensing some cockiness.

"So," Nicole began when they settled into their seats. "This seems to be your spot."
She did her best to keep her tone light and not sarcastic, which Chelle told her to work on.
"Yeah. This is like one of the hotspots in Miami right now. You know you're gonna see somebody when you come up in here," he replied.
"And you enjoy that? Being seen and what not."
"I guess it comes with the lifestyle. I get recog-

nized most places I go, so I might as well go where I'm not the only standout. Like tonight. You got an actress sitting to your left, and a couple of Miami Heat players behind you." He gestured behind her and gave the party in question a head nod. Being nosey, she turned to see which players it was, and saw Jay sitting at the table with them. He grinned and raised his glass to her. She smiled weakly and turned back to Vance.

Of course, she would go out on a date and Jay would be in the same damn restaurant. If her odds got any worse, they'd be evens. Again, Nicole fought to keep her composure and smiled at Vance who was assessing her curiously.

"You know Jay Montgomery?" He seemed incredulous that she would know anyone famous other than him.

"Yeah. We went to college together. He's also close to Dom."

"Ah. Got it. I didn't think you'd been down here long enough to get in the mix like that."

Nicole frowned. "What do you mean?"

"You know. The mix. The chicks who date the ballers or celebs," he replied.

"Oh, I see."

Nicole figured that what he'd said wasn't great, but to hear him explain it was even worse. She had the feeling of being on a rollercoaster on a slow downhill descent. Not wanting to count him out yet, she opted to see if he had any redeeming qualities.

Their server came to take their drink order. Before Nicole could even open her mouth, Vance requested bottle service like they were in the VIP section of a club. She wondered how much he planned on drinking to need an entire bottle of Grey Goose.

"I'll have a mango margarita, please," she requested.
"You don't like Goose?" Vance asked.
"I'm not a huge vodka drinker. I like tequila and good champagne."
"It's cool," he shrugged. "By the time we finish networking, this bottle will be done."
"Networking?"
"Well, that's what I call it. But I know a few people coming through, so they'll have drinks with us, and whoever else wanna chill."
"Isn't that what clubs are for?" She was grasping at straws now, trying not to trip. At that point, she just wanted to have some good food and chalk the night up to getting her feet wet in the dating pool.
"Yeah, but clubs have too many regular people clamoring for your attention and staring all night."
Regular people?
"They also don't have five-star sushi," Ni-

cole added. She'd been perusing the menu and couldn't wait to try some of the selections.

"Nah, I don't really fuck with sushi. I'll probably have the steak or something," he said, and she noticed he never even cracked the menu open.

"Hmmm," she hummed because she didn't want to ask, 'who comes to a sushi restaurant if they don't eat sushi?' in a tone that let him know she thought he was an idiot. He essentially brought her here to parade her around and hang out with whoever he knew. Were they even on a date?

In the middle of her wandering thoughts, his phone rang, and he answered it. Whoever it was seemed to be doing all the talking on the other line. She glanced around the crowd, trying to focus on something so that she wasn't staring into his mouth. The hairs on the back of her neck were prickly and her instincts sensed that if she turned around Jay would be looking at her. When she did, he didn't even try to conceal the amusement on his face. He looked away, focusing back on the conversation at his table.

After a few terse directives, Vance got off his call and put his phone, face down, on the table. There was no apology for taking the call and he began to grumble about how long it was taking them to bring out the drinks. Nicole was finding it increasingly harder to stay positive and upbeat. The slick remarks were begging her to unleash on him, but part of her wanted things to turn around more than anything.

"So, Miss. Nicole. Tell me about yourself. I want to know what makes you tick."

Nicole cleared her throat. She really needed that drink if she was going to get through the night.

"Well, I'm from New York. I went to FAMU which is how I met Kiko, Dom, and Jay, and now I'm down here work –"
"Shit," Vance hissed as he glared down at his phone that was buzzing nonstop on the table. He picked it up, rolled his neck to the side and looked at it. "I'll be right back. I've got to take this."

Nicole couldn't even fake being surprised that he left her sitting at the table. As he walked toward the bar area, the server arrived with their drinks.

"Bless you," she said before taking a healthy sip of her drink.
"You look like you're having fun," Jay said as he slipped into one of the empty seats at the table.
"Time of my life," Nicole drawled as she raised her glass to him.
"I tried to help you out, but you didn't want to tell me who you met. Could have saved you this headache," he chuckled.
"Well, I'll be sure to put you on retainer for next time."

Before Jay could respond, Vance returned to the table. The two men greeted, and Jay nodded toward the bottle of vodka.

"Looks like you bout to get it in tonight. We doin' shots?"

Nicole glared at him like he was insane, wondering what his angle was besides making her night even worse.

"Hell, yeah," Vance replied. Whoever had just called seemed to have stressed him out a bit. He poured out the two shots and handed one to Jay.

"What about you, Nicole?" Jay began to grab a shot glass for her, but she placed her hand over his to stop him. If she didn't know any better, she would have sworn a lightning bolt shot straight to her core from the warmth of his hand.

"I'm drinking Tequila," she explained.

"Oh, well then let's get you some."

Jay motioned for their server as Vance looked on, slightly perturbed. After ordering a bottle, he turned to Vance and asked about a mutual friend. Nicole was grateful for the distraction and sipped her drink in peace as the two men chatted. She had no idea why Jay ordered an entire bottle of tequila, but she was just along for the ride.

When it came, Jay fixed Nicole a shot and they

all toasted to good health and then tossed them back.

"Alright, man. Thanks for the shot. You two enjoy your night," Jay said as he stood to leave.

"Ok, man. Good to see you again," Vance replied and shook his hand.

"See you around, Nicole."

"Yep. See ya," she replied, barely able to contain her disappointment that her buffer was leaving.

"Jay's a cool dude. It's fucked up what happened with him and the Heat, but I heard he's doing well for himself, and almost healthy enough to play again," Vance said.

Nicole wanted to ask him what he meant by that remark, but before she could, a woman's loud voice came screeching toward their table. Nicole looked up just in time to see a tall, thick Latino woman yelling at Vance and pointing in his face.

"So, you are out with another bitch!"

Stunned, Nicole gaped at the woman who was dressed in leggings, a crop top, and Ugg Boots. Her long curly hair was pulled up in a messy bun, and she seemed like she was primed for a good tussle.

"Letty! Chill. This is just a friend. Why you always acting crazy?"

"You a damn lie!" Letty yelled as she grabbed the bottle of vodka out of the bucket.

"Whoa," Nicole said as she pushed her chair away from the table.

The manager was already approaching to remove the uninvited guest, but she wasn't gonna sit there if this girl was ready to attack. Just as she was getting up, Letty began pouring the liquor all over Vance who was trying to snatch it away from her. He jumped up, finally succeeding, and she began swinging on him.

Just then, Nicole was whisked away from the table as Jay grabbed her and her purse and led her out of the restaurant. Once outside, he steadied her on her feet, and they stopped to listen to the commotion inside. They exchanged a long glance, Nicole with wide surprised eyes, and Jay squinting with annoyance, that slowly morphed into amusement then they burst out laughing. She doubled over as her mind replayed the startled look on Vance's face when he was being doused with vodka.

 The sound of Letty yelling "Get the fuck off me," getting closer and closer snapped them out of it and Jay grabbed her hand. "Let's get out of here before the drama makes its way outside."

"That was a mess," Nicole thought out loud as Jay ordered them two shots of tequila from a bar not too far from the restaurant and the failed date he had just rescued her from.

"I think mess is putting it lightly," he replied.

"Ok. How about a fuggin' disaster?"

He nodded. "That's more like it. I could have told you about Vance and his secret baby mamas."

"*Mamas?* Plural? How many are there?"

"Well," Jay thought about it. "There are two, including Letty, that have popped up on his ass before, and he's rumored to have one in Atlanta."

"Are you kidding me? How did Kiko or Dom not warn me?"

"In Dom's defense, he probably didn't know. He doesn't really socialize with the single guys, and I know this from a friend of one of the baby mamas."

"A chick, I'm assuming," Nicole said, dryly.

She didn't know why that seemed to irk her nerves. Jay raised a brow at her tone but didn't address it. The bartender placed two shot glasses in front of them and poured a generous serving of Clase Azul in each one. Jay pushed one toward Nicole and grabbed one for himself.

"Here's to better dates," Jay toasted, raising his shot in the air.

"Here's to men who can be faithful without psycho baby mama drama," Nicole added.

Jay chuckled before tossing back his drink. Nicole followed suit and grimaced while the liquor burned on its way down.

"Smooth," she gritted between her teeth."

Jay signaled for another round.

"But at what point did the date start going downhill for you?"
"Hmm... I think maybe when he assumed I was in 'the mix' and his explanation of what that meant when I had no clue."

Jay shook his head. "Vance is a cool guy to hang out with, but his money has definitely gone to his head. But that mixy shit is South Beach. Everyone is trying to get next to anyone they think will elevate them in some way. You have people, women and men, who date the older millionaires who finance their lifestyle while they mingle with the 'in crowd' trying to find someone."
"Sounds lovely." Nicole scoffed as she recalled the way Vance discussed the women in his particular social circle.
"Like I said. There are certain people who subscribe to that shit, but you're not in that category and as you can see, they're easy to spot."

"Are you in that category?"

Jay shrugged, marking her with an incredulous glare. "Me?"

"I mean, do you date women like that?"

"No."

"Ok. You said that fast as hell."

"Because I don't. It's simple. I learned in college to watch out for girls like that. I have too many options to scrape the bottom of the barrel."

"Excuse me!"

"I mean think about it. You have the choice between ten men. Would you pick the one that you knew only wanted to use you? I know a lot of guys who don't care and will abuse that ass. I don't have the patience for that shit. I have to at least enjoy the company of any woman I'm dealing with on any level."

Nicole nodded. Based on her conversations with Chelle and Kiko, and his explanation, she was developing a whole new perspective on Jay. "What are you thinking about," he asked, lightly tapping her temple.

"I'm adjusting my mental image of you," she answered.

"From what to what?"

"Well... From being a dog," she wrinkled her nose.

"Wow." He seemed disappointed.

"Don't wow me. You know how you got down in school. There would practically be a line of girls waiting to talk to you after a game, or when we were at parties. You had a different chick on your arm every weekend, sometimes two."

"Yeah. I fucked with a lot of girls, but I wasn't lying to or cheating on anyone, and I didn't have any drama."

"You're right. In my head, though, that's what I imagined."

"That's fucked up." Jay shook his head. "So, what about now?"

"I don't know," she smirked. "I kinda like what I'm uncovering."

"I wish you would uncover it," he murmured. Nicole shot him an impassive glance.

"I bet you do."

"So, now that you've wasted your time with a dude like Vance, it's my time."

"Your time?" Nicole laughed. "Your time for what, exactly?"

"My time," he leaned forward and tipped her chin up toward him, "to show you how a real man behaves."

His voice deepened to that tone that had her squeezing her thighs together on the barstool. The way he could switch a gear and dominate her with a velvet glove over iron fist energy. He was usually so unassuming that when he became bold and direct, it did something to her inside.

"Jay, quit it." She tried to brush his suggestion off as a joke, but he didn't grin or release her when she attempted to bat his hand away from her face.

"I'm serious. Let me take you out on a date." His eyes burned with an indescribable invitation that she was almost ready to accept.

"What are you scared of?" He asked when she hesitated to respond to him.

"We're friends. I don't want to mess that up."

He released a low growl of frustration. "A date Nicole. One date. Unless you're scared that it will lead to more dates and what that might lead to."

"Stop saying I'm scared."

"Then stop acting scared."

"I'm not acting scared. I'm being careful. I'm starting a new chapter in my life and my focus is on learning who I am outside of a relationship. I plan on dating multiple people and enjoy the process of discovering what I do and don't like."

"And I respect that. But it's interesting that me dating multiple people makes me a dog, but for you it's self-discovery."

"I said dating multiple people, not fucking multiple people."

"For the record, I did not fuck every girl that I dated, or was seen with back in the day."

"Noted."

"And fine. Date multiple people and fuck me."

She cackled at that. "Jay, be serious!"

He reached forward, placing a hand on the side of each of her thighs. Nicole held her breath, waiting to see what he would do next. Gripping her stool, he dragged it forward until she was in between his long legs, then slid his hands back to the top of her thighs. The light pressure he applied as he grasped and released her flesh ignited a four-alarm blaze between her legs.

"Be honest." He surveyed her face, admiring her beauty as he decided on what approach to take with her. Leaning forward, he placed his lips close to her ear and asked, "Do you want me?"

Nicole's eyes fluttered, and she inhaled a slow, deep breath attempting to compose herself, which didn't work because of his magnetizing scent. "What do you mean?"

"Do you want me?" He enunciated. "When I touch you, does your body react? If I could slide my fingers across, what I imagine to be, your pretty kitty cat, would it be wet?" He tiptoed his fingers upwards as he spoke, and she was squirming in her seat as her body came alive under his touch.

"Yes," she uttered, biting her lip.

"The other night, after the party, didn't you wish I had kissed you?" His fingers crept along a path that seemed to be headed to forbidden territory. Nicole's breathing increased as she imagined Jay teasing her with no clothes on.

"Maybe," she breathed out.

He switched ears. "Yes," he corrected her.

His hands were at the apex of her thighs, and he splayed his long fingers wide, sliding his thumbs in between her legs. Nicole placed her hands over his to halt his progress. She couldn't take much more. "Does it scare you how much you want me? Because sometimes I can't believe how bad I want you."

"I don't know if I'm ready for that," she whispered.

"I think you are ready, but I won't push you," he said and kissed her ear. "One date. That's all I ask."

Straightening up, Jay leveled her with a sultry glance before he slammed his second shot home. He gestured for her to do the same, and she did, noting the second one went down much easier. Nicole couldn't help but simper under his gaze. "What are you doing to me?"

The corners of his mouth curved upwards, and he winked. "You need to have some fun. C'mon. Let's go."

Chapter 9

Fifteen minutes later they were walking into the karaoke spot. Nicole had recognized it immediately when their taxi pulled up in front. For the first time, she didn't make any assumptions as to where things would lead, or what might happen. Maybe it was the tequila, but she felt relaxed and ready to have a good time. And hungry.

"I'm starving," she groaned.

"Oh, that's right," Jay chuckled. "You didn't even make it to appetizers before your episode of cheaters started."

"Ha ha," she snorted. "I was looking forward to trying their sushi, too."

"Aww, man. Their food is amazing. Like, delectable."

"Thanks for rubbing it in!"

"Don't worry. You'll have it soon. But the sushi here is decent, too. It should hold you over."

"I'll take your word for it."

Their server came to take their drink and food order. Jay ordered a bottle of tequila she'd never heard of before, and pineapple juice as a chaser, which she was good with.

"I'll have a spicy yellowtail roll, and the volcano, but I'll start with an order of gyoza, and chicken tempura. Thank you." She handed her menu to the server, catching Jay's amused expression before he placed his order, which was like hers except for the addition of a spider crab roll, and Japanese fried rice.

"What's so funny?" She asked when she had his attention again.

"Just admiring your healthy appetite. You have no idea how many women order a Caesar salad as an entree. If they do order a full meal, they take a few bites and then wrap it up."

"That's crazy. If I'm hungry, I eat. I'm not thick on accident."

"I know that's right," he murmured, and Nicole smirked.

"Whatever."

They continued to chat and joke around through their dinner, and the bottle of tequila had them both feeling nice. Nicole blamed her giggling at everything he said, on that. While they ate, other patrons were performing their favorite songs and Nicole danced along in her seat, happy that her night had turned around. Contrary to her previous delve into denial, Jay was a lot of fun to be around, and she felt comfortable with him. She was getting into a jazzy rendition of Real Love by Mary J Blige when she saw two familiar faces approaching the table.

Kiko couldn't hold back the look of sheer amazement at finding Nicole with Jay when she was supposed to be with Vance. Mallory was trying but failing not to make it obvious that she knew something was up between them. Her gaze kept flitting from Jay and smirking when she looked at Nicole.

"Hey guys," Nicole said cheerily, and Kiko's eyes widened in bewilderment.
"What's happening here?"
"Just a friendly dinner," Jay explained. "Join us." He offered them drinks with a jiggle of the tequila bottle.
"Um?" Mallory was flabbergasted.
"We're meeting some more friends," Kiko re-

plied.

"The more the merrier," Jay bellowed.

"C'mon. Sit!"

Nicole patted a chair next to her. The way the dining area was set up, you could pull several small tables together to accommodate larger parties. The two newcomers settled in, and Jay instructed them to order whatever they wanted on his tab. Kiko kept throwing furtive glances at Nicole, noticing how comfortable she seemed with her companion for the evening.

"I feel like there's an elephant in the room," Mallory finally spoke up.

"Yeah. I didn't want to say anything, but weren't you supposed to be elsewhere tonight?" Kiko asked, sounding perplexed.

"You mean her date with Vance?" Jay scoffed. "You may need to employ a team of fact checkers if you plan on throwing anymore singles mixers."

"What?" Kiko let out a nervous chuckle.

"He's got a baby mama factory," Nicole blabbed. "Just cranking them out."

"What is going on?" Mallory asked Kiko since it was obvious that Jay and Nicole were in their own little world.

"Girl..." Kiko would have been concerned if she wasn't so glad to see Nicole having fun for a change.

"It's like someone snatched Nicole and replaced her with this... lady," Mallory said under her breath.

"I can hear you *biatches*," Nicole cackled. "And there's nothing wrong with me, since Jay rescued me from that dumpster fire of a date."

"Will one of you tell me what the hell happened?" Kiko attempted to get them to focus because curiosity was killing her.

"Vance was horrible," Nicole blurted out. "He was shallow and just... ugh. But I was hungry, so I tried to push through. Well next thing, baby mama came through spilling drinks and throwin 'bows."

Kiko and Mallory both gaped at the story Nicole rushed through.

"His baby mama showed up? I didn't even know he had kids!"

"Issa secret," Nicole whispered, placing a finger over her lips, and Jay laughed at her dramatics.

"Yeah," Jay confirmed. "From what I heard, he has about three. This particular one, rolled up in Zuma ready to throw down. I had to get Nick up out of there before she even thought about touching her."

"Yep. Snatched me right up off my feet and carried me outside," Nicole added.

"Is this a real story? Because... *Damn!*" Mallory

grabbed the tequila and carafe of pineapple juice to make herself a stiff drink. "I have some catching up to do, I see."

"Pass the liquor over here," Kiko said as she made one for herself. "So, Vance's baby mama showed up to your date? I can't... That can't be true."

"Letty," Nicole said. "She looks like she be beatin' the breaks off his ass, too. The look on his face when she started swinging!" Nicole dissolved into a fit of giggles, and Jay egged her on, laughing.

"Nah," he chuckled. "When she doused him in vodka, for a split second I thought she was gonna strike a match and flambé that man!" He let out a deep throaty laugh that caught the attention of the tables around them, and caused Nicole to fold over onto the table in a drunken fit of giggles.

"I am weak!" She cried out, and Kiko and Mallory couldn't help but join them.

"That's friggin' hilarious," Mallory chirped.

"Wait til I tell Dom," Kiko giggled.

"Yeah. No more footballers for me," Nicole said, blotting tears from the corners of her eyes. Kiko didn't miss the fleeting expression of disdain that swept across Jay's features before he schooled them into a relaxed grin. Nicole's comment had struck a nerve.

Soon, Kiko's WAG friends arrived. She introduced them all to Nicole, and promoted the article she had done for Kiko's wedding. Eventually, the conversation returned to Vance, and Nicole and Jay had the entire table cracking up as they retold the story, adding details they missed the first time. Jay made sure to keep Nicole's drink refreshed and after a while she was good and tipsy.

"Ok," Kiko said. "Who's gonna sing?"
Everyone looked around the table, no one wanting to be the first person up. Nicole avoided Jay's eyes by staring into her drink as she stirred it, but that didn't work.
"Nicole," he sang. "I think you owe me, turtle dove!"
"I do not owe you anything! I said maybe."
"Turtle dove?" Mallory giggled.
"C'mon, Nick! You should do it. We both did it last time," Kiko whined.
"Ok! I'll do it." Nicole pushed her seat back and stood up, feeling fine, she strode toward the DJ to make her selection. She browsed through the catalog looking for something that would complement her raspy voice and lower register. It was either going to be TBoz or Toni Braxton. A devilish grin spread across her face when she turned to "Red Light Special" by TLC. She handed the DJ the booklet of songs and headed to the stage.

The sexy chords of the electric guitar at the beginning of the track set the mood as Nicole swayed her hips, her natural dancer instincts kicking in. She strutted around the stage, making eye contact with the audience, and found Jay's eyes glued to her. When she began to sing in a raspy tone similar to TBoz, a few catcalls and whistles rang out.

She worked it, seducing the crowd with her body and sensuous timbre of her voice. Taking her time, she made her way toward Jay. No matter where she went or what her body did, he was her point of reference. When she stood in front of him, he bit his lip as he smiled up at her. Turning her back on him, she sung the chorus while dancing suggestively, glancing over her shoulder to watch his reaction.

It took every ounce of restraint Jay had to keep his hands to himself, and he dug his fingers into the fabric of his jeans. He wanted to pull her down onto his lap so she could feel just what she was doing to him. He'd seen her dance a million times before, but there was something about that song, and the look in her eyes that had him feeling like he couldn't breathe. There was a sense that she was setting him up for the kill, and all he could do was sit there and wait for it.

Nicole continued singing, not facing him, stalking side to side like a pantheress. Changing up her tone a bit, she sang the chorus as an alto instead of a tenor. She was an ok singer if she stayed in the right range, and she gave it her all. The cheers and claps she received let her know she was killing it.

There were a few single men in the audience that looked like they wished they were in Jay's seat. She smiled and winked at a couple, really feeling herself at that point. When she faced him, Jay's eyes were smoldering. Feeling wicked, Nicole shoved his shoulder, pushing him back in the chair as she straddled him, one leg at a time. Kiko and Mallory both gasped with shock at how naughty she was, and how hot the couple looked together.

Nicole didn't skip a beat, continuing to roll and rock her body, a master at the art of seduction. Her calculated movements as she simulated a heated riding session, had the desired effect of looking poised and erotic. She was teasing and titillating, fiery yet coy, and she had Jay wrapped around her finger. He was totally locked in on her to where his breathing was synchronized with hers. The look he gave her spoke volumes, and it screamed sex.

There was a part in the song where Chili sang

about being a real woman who knew who she was, and what she wanted, Nicole became aggressive. She grabbed Jay's chin and stared him in the eyes as she sang. Then she roughly let him go and pushed off his lap in one smooth motion. She finished the song by sauntering to the mic stand.

When she was done, she received a standing ovation.

Returning to the table, she received another round of applause from her friends. Kiko stood up and gave her a high five, yelling, "That's my girl," as she pointed at Nicole, and Mallory mimicked bowing down to her. Jay had the same mischievous smile plastered on his face.

"Cat got your tongue?" Nicole taunted him.
"You definitely did your thing," he said. The way his eyes bored into her, Nicole felt naked and exposed. Jay had a quiet intensity to him that simmered beneath the surface. On the outside, he seemed calm, but she could sense the danger lurking. She had poked the beast.

At the end of the night, they all gathered in front of the lounge as everyone coordinated their way home. Those who drove retrieved their cars from valet, and those who had car services hopped in and left. Nicole didn't have a way home planned because Vance had picked her up. Kiko offered to order her a car, but Jay was against it.

"Nick has had too much to drink. I'll have my driver drop her off."

"Ok. That works for me," Kiko was quick to agree, hugging them both before getting in her ride-share with Mallory.

"I'm fine," Nicole objected, but the fact that she was swaying said otherwise.

"Sure," Jay replied. He was tipsy too, but he wasn't going to be satisfied unless he saw her enter her front door.

The car ride was quiet as they both succumbed to their own thoughts. Jay was feeling drunker by the minute and hoped he'd be ok when they arrived at her place. Nicole was thinking she should get her key ready so she wouldn't have to fumble with it, but after she took it out of her purse, she forgot why she had it in her hand and put it back. When the driver pulled into her driveway, they both breathed a sigh of relief.

Jay slid out of his side of the car and walked around to open her door, helping Nicole to her feet. When she giggled for no reason, he chuckled. With a hand at her back, he guided her to her doorstep. She fumbled in her bag for her keys, again, and made a big deal of showing him she found them. Placing her back to the door for support, she smiled up at him.

"I guess this is goodnight," she purred.

"Is it?" Jay leaned over her, one hand on the door above her head, and the other smoothing a few loose strands of hair out of her face. Nicole inhaled at his touch, breathing in his scent, and releasing her pent-up lust as she breathed out.

"Jay," she groaned, but when he nuzzled her neck, she didn't push him away. "What are you doing?"

"I wanna kiss," he said, dragging his lips up her neck.

"Nooo," she drawled, turning her head to the side. "Not on the lips."

"Why not the lips?"

"Because. It will go too far," she whimpered but Jay didn't care.

He was too busy kissing her everywhere else. Her chin, her collar bone, the deep groove of her throat, and where the corner of her lips met her cheeks. He felt the struggle as her body fluctuated between being tense and on guard and relaxed and submissive. As bad as he wanted her, he wouldn't push beyond what she was comfortable with.

"Is this too much? Tell me what you want."

"I want," she began, but then hissed when he kissed her ear. "Can you just stay with me? No sex. Just be here with me?"

The liquor had loosened her up to being able to exhibit her loneliness. It was a moment of weakness to her, but to Jay it made him adore her even more.

"Ok," he agreed, even though his dick was harder than a brick.

Signaling for his driver to go, Jay followed Nicole inside. They fumbled through her house in darkness until she reached her bedroom and turned on a warm bedside lamp. It wasn't very bright and set the room in an amber glow, casting shadows leading away from her bed into the corners.

Jay watched her as she struggled to remove her dress and stepped forward to help her. Unzipping the back, he pulled her arms out of the off-shoulder sleeves while she wobbled on her feet, and her head lolled to the side. As much as he would have loved to enjoy seeing her half-naked, he knew the signs of someone on the verge of passing out and Nicole was there. Not knowing where her pajamas were, he improvised and pulled off his shirt and slipped it over her head.

"Smells so good," she breathed as she lurched toward the bed, tumbling onto it, and rolling from side to side until she found a comfortable spot. Jay stripped down to his boxers and climbed into bed next to her, turning off the lamp and fluffing the pillows under his head to his liking. Nicole sighed beside him and reached her hand out for his. He took her hand in his and placed it on his chest. It wasn't how he envisioned his night ending, but for some reason, he was content.

Chapter 10

I t was still dark when Nicole's eyes fluttered open. She was still a bit woozy, but
she was comfortable. A little bit *too* comfortable, and it took her a moment to realize that
she was snuggly enclosed in Jay's embrace, and
that it was her arm that was keeping him pinned
there. She almost shoved him away, as she normally would, but it had been so long since she
had cuddled. It felt... Nice.

There was no harm in enjoying the moment,
right?

Thinking back to the events of the night before,
she vaguely recalled him slipping his shirt over
her head and climbing into bed. She wasn't sure
how they wound up in the position they were in,
but she didn't want to breathe too deep so much

as to alert him that she might be awake. Instead, she chose to bask in the secure feeling of his body against hers, and his masculine chocolate musk scent. As much as she hated to admit it, Jay was sexy as hell, and it turned her on.

Didn't mean she wanted anything from him, and this moment of weakness was a wakeup call that she needed to get her head together. Nicole thought of all the ways Jay could turn this into an opportunity to torment her in the future, and she tried to devise the best way to get out from under him. She was drifting back to sleep when he pressed his face into the back of her neck, nose tickling her skin, and inhaled.

"Why are you *sniffing* me?" She couldn't even help herself. She was so used to calling out his every move that she forgot her own agenda. She attempted to push his arm away, but he hugged her tighter.

"Why are you pretending to be asleep?" The way his deep Barry White-esque voice danced across her eardrums made her quiver with lust as he cradled her to him.

"You woke me up," she lied. The last thing she wanted was for Jay to know that she actually enjoyed him holding her. It didn't matter though; he was already calling her bluff by pressing gentle kisses along the back of her neck. As if daring her to tell him to stop.

"Sure," he hummed against her ear. When she didn't protest, he kissed it, snaking his tongue out to trace the outline of the delicate skin. He couldn't resist.

Nicole found herself frozen. Caught between wanting to curse his existence and submitting to the intense tingling between her legs. Caught in the careful web he'd spun, just for her. All the years of his constant flirting chipping away at her defenses. Despite her most logical efforts, her body wanted more of what Jay was teasing her with.

"Jay," she groaned. Her carnal desires had sparked to life, and the promise of where things could go was torturing her. Her skin was on fire wherever he touched, and her pussy was on full blaze. Jay continued kissing and licking her ear until she was gripping the sheets in agony. She shouldn't want him, but she did, and the tsunami between her legs told the true story.

Jay, feeling the heat rising between them, was trying but failing to hold back. It had been hard enough sleeping in the same bed with Nicole, bathing in her scent, and listening to her soft breathing until he finally fell asleep. He'd woken to her tossing and turning and had been on high alert from the moment she sighed in her sleep and snuggled her luscious ass against him. Attempting to be a gentleman, he scooted away but then her body sought him out and her arm kept him in place.

His dick had been on hard ever since, and he was struggling not to press it into her, until she shuddered against him, and he saw her fingers grasping the sheets. Nicole couldn't hide the fact that she wanted him, and he wasn't going to let her. Not after wanting her for so long. His desire for her was coiled tight, and his excitement at her unexpected submission fueled his advances. The arm around her waist held her tighter and he began to caress her thighs, sliding his hand slowly upward, grasping and squeezing her soft flesh along the way. Nicole pressed her face into the pillows, releasing the faintest whimper at his touch.

Without words, she encouraged him to continue with her body language. She pressed her thigh against his hand, urging for more contact. Jay groaned, grinding his hard length into the yielding flesh of her thick ass. The pleasure from easing the intense pressure causing him to hiss against her neck, sending shockwaves through her body. "Jay," she moaned.

Nicole was beyond pretending, and her body was begging her to let something, anything happen. At the very least, she needed something to take the edge off. When she felt the size of his erection poking her, everything happened at once.

Her nipples ached to be touched, her clit pulsed for attention, and her pussy throbbed to be filled. Without thinking, she grabbed his hand and pressed it between her legs, grinding against him at the initial burst of pleasure.

"Damn, Fat Ma," Jay whispered harshly as he palmed her plump mound. He followed her lead and massaged her through her panties, finding the fabric already soaked. "Shit," he groaned as he slipped his fingers under the seam until he slid up against her clit. Nicole bucked and gasped at that slight contact.

When he began to rub her in a circular motion she strained into his touch, and his hips began to involuntarily match the rhythm as he humped her from behind. Jay wanted to rip her panties off and give her the back shots of her life, but somehow sensed that he needed to take his time. He may have had the reputation of a player, but nothing about wanting Nicole was a game.

So, he continued to fondle her, with a mounting case of blue balls threatening to take him out. Nicole had a death grip on his arm as she rode his hand. When he pressed his thumb to her clit and slid his middle finger into her dripping center, they both groaned. Nicole from the verge of an orgasm, and Jay for imagining what it would feel like to slide his dick inside her.

"Look at you, soaked," he murmured. "You

wanna come so bad, don't you? Do you need two fingers?"

The question was rhetorical because he was already inserting another finger inside her as he applied more pressure from his hand and body.

"*Ahh*!" Nicole found herself completely under his spell. If he would have told her to bark like a dog, she would have.

"I know, baby. You're close. So close. Keep squeezing my fingers with your hot little pussy."

Nicole closed her eyes shut tight, the sound of his smooth vocals pushing her into a delicious tailspin. Her back arched and she cried out as an orgasm ricocheted through her. Her body shook as wave after wave took her breath away, and her thighs trapped his hand in a vice grip as she clamped them together.

"Oh, Nicky," he uttered the forbidden nickname into her shoulder. "That's my girl. Relax. Let me take care of you."

Jay resumed placing soft kisses along her shoulder, up her neck, across her cheeks and to the corner of her lips. Even though he knew he had her right where he wanted her, part of him needed Nicole to verbally submit to taking things further. He waited for her to turn her head so that he could have access to more of her lush lips.

He could have easily taken her from behind. Slid her thong to the side and banged one home, but that wasn't what he wanted. Just being inside her wasn't enough. He wanted all of her. Her kisses, her sex faces, and he wanted to feel wanted.

Still seeing stars, Nicole realized that instead of easing her desire, Jay's touch had opened her Pandora's box, literally, and she needed more. Wanted more. As he urged her to relax, she shut her mind off, and became as ready and willing as her body. Instead of turning her head, she rolled her entire body around to face him. Parting her lips to accept his kiss.

"Tell me you want me," Jay demanded. He looked into her eyes, searching for *something*... They shared a moment, where that familiar unspoken sentiment transpired between them, where his feelings were finally reciprocated. Nicole hesitated to answer, and he nipped her full bottom lip.

"I fuckin' want you," she whispered.

His mouth crashed against hers as he finally kissed her the way he'd been wanting to for so long. Hot and passionate turned into hungry and chaotic as years of pent-up longing unfurled. He suckled her lips and slid his tongue into her mouth, roughly sucking hers into his. Licking and lashing her tongue with his until she was writhing against him.

Jay grabbed handfuls of her ass, rolling onto his back as he pulled her on top of him. He pumped his hips upward wanting nothing more than to push past her flimsy barrier and inside of her. Nicole kissed him back just as passionately as he did her, surprising him with her intensity. The way she was rocking her hips had him feeling like he was going to come through his shorts.

"Touch me." His command sounded like a plea as he became desperate for her.

Nicole splayed her hands across his chest, smiling before she began to slide them lower. Slowly, she explored the ridges and planes of his muscular form, grasping his hips, and then shoved her hand inside his boxers.

"Ooh," she gasped, eyes wide. Biting her lip, she explored his shaft from root to tip while he gloated over her surprised reaction. If she would have known the anaconda that Jay possessed between his legs, she might have given him a chance years ago. His thickness filled up her hand to where her fingers barely touched. He groaned into her mouth when she began, pumping her fist.

Jay peeled away her clothes, and she removed his boxers in return. When her breasts swung free from her bra, his mouth watered and he leaned forward, slurping a nipple like he was sampling a ripe fruit. Nicole threw her head back and moaned wildly. She loved his enthusiasm and sound effects. Something about Jay made her come alive. He just seemed to know what she wanted and how she wanted it.

Holding onto her waist, he lifted her as he finally pulled her panties away. He slid his hand back between her thighs, finding her sweet spot swimming with her essence. The loud squishy sounds his fingers made when he fingered her made his dick jump.

"Come sit on my face, love." He urged her toward his head, supporting her thighs as she scooted forward on his command.

"Oh, God," Nicole moaned when he pushed his mouth into her and pulled her full weight onto him. His lips and tongue devoured her like she was a melting push-pop, and the fact that it was Jay doing this to her made it all the more elicit. She grabbed the top of the headboard, balancing on her knees so that she could ride his face.

Jay couldn't believe that he was finally with Nicole, and it had been more than worth the wait. He couldn't believe how good she tasted, and lapped her up, moaning as her juices dripped down his chin. His erection was throbbing out of control, and he gripped it, rubbing his pre-cum over the head. He knew he needed to come because if he waited until he was inside her, it'd be game over. Fast. His hard-on was damn near ten years in the making and getting that first nut out the way so that he could focus when he was finally up in her, was necessary.

So, he began stroking himself as he enjoyed the sweet taste of her pussy and the beautiful sound of her moans and whimpers. Nicole felt Jay's body shifting beneath her and looked back to see the sight of his taut muscles and veins popping out of his forearm as his hand gripped and stroked his length. It turned her on, incredibly, even more. Getting an idea, she lifted off Jay's face, ignoring his protest as she turned around, placing her pussy back on his lips as she leaned forward.

While he stroked, she placed wet kisses on the tip of his rock-hard erection. Then she wrapped her lips around the smooth head and began to suck as he lifted his hips toward her. Nicole sucked, and cupped his balls and he began to shudder beneath her. His moans vibrated through her core as he let go, spilling into her mouth while she continued to suck him dry.

"Got-*damn*," he uttered, turning his head to the side and gasping for air as she kept her pace. Usually, he would have needed a few minutes to recover, but Nicole was doing some sort of sorcery, and his dick was responding to her touch.

Jay's head fell back into the pillow as she continued her onslaught. He relaxed, winding his fingers into her hair to steady her. He didn't want to come in her mouth again, just needed to be hard enough to slip inside her. When he was there, he used his other hand to pull his dick away.

Nicole wiped the corners of her mouth with her fingers and turned back around to face him. Jay was looking at her like a man who was about to go to war, and it thrilled her. She already knew she was in for a one hell of a ride.

Holding his shaft, Jay rested the other hand on her hip as she lowered onto him. It had been a while for her, and her tightness and his size were a tricky combination, but she didn't let that deter her. Inch by inch, she slid down onto him as he filled and stretched her to her limits. He urged her upper body toward him so that he could kiss and caress her breasts, and Nicole moaned deeply at the overload of sensations.

When she was so full of him that she could hardly move, Jay gripped her hips and started rocking her as he made small thrusts to push even deeper into her.

"Jay, please," she cried out at the overwhelming sensation of him touching every sensitive spot all at once. Jay continued a lazy circular grinding of his waist as he waited for her body to adjust to him. He enjoyed the expression of agony on her face even as she whimpered his name and begged him not to stop.

"That's it, baby," he crooned when she began to match his movements. "Fuck me back."

He increased his pace until she was bouncing on top of him. Soon she threw her head back and rode him like she was on a mechanical bull. The sexy sway of her body as she rocked and rolled him had Jay biting his lip. Nicole was as excellent a dancer on his dick as she was on the dance floor.

"*Mmhm*. Ride that dick, Nicky," he encouraged her.
"Mmmm," was her response. She was floating into another dimension with the intensity of the orgasm that was budding in her core. Her eyes fixed on his face, drinking in every twitch of his lips or eyebrows as he enjoyed the ride.

Jay felt the familiar fire kindling in the base of his spine, and while he could have probably fucked her for another hour without stopping, he was ready to hear her scream his name. With a sudden move, he swept her up in his arms and flipped her onto her back without ever pulling out. Nicole squeaked in surprise and then groaned when began to fuck her senseless. With one hand, he grabbed both of hers and pinned them behind her head. The other hand pushed one of her thighs back so that he could enter her more deeply.

"Say my name," he gritted between his teeth. Nicole thrashed her head from side to side, overcome with pleasure.

"No?" Jay grunted. He did a swirl motion and then repeated it at a pace that she thought wasn't possible to maintain without faltering, but he did, hitting a spot that made her cry out each time until she couldn't hold back.

"Jay!" She moaned loudly as she came even harder while he continued to drive his dick into her. Again and again until he began to shake, bracing himself with one arm as his dam burst.

"Fuck," he uttered in a drawn-out groan. His head fell back, his body suspended until his dick stopped pulsing and he tumbled onto his side next to her.

The fact that he'd just had his way with Nicole, and she was laid out next to him having trouble breathing had Jay feeling like he was king of the world. Nicole was trying to regain her breath and her senses while processing the fact that she'd gone there with him. Everything that he'd always promised; that he'd rock her world and have her screaming his name was true, and she'd fallen into his trap quite easily.

"I can't believe that just happened," she whispered.

"Me either," he purred, turning to face her. He snaked an arm around her waist, pulling her closer and nuzzling her neck. He wasn't sure if things had changed between them, or if it was a one-time thing so he wasn't going to waste his opportunity. "But I'm ready to do it again," he murmured against her skin.

Nicole shuddered, his words aligning with the current of desire zinging through her body. Wrapping her arms around his neck, she opened her legs to accommodate him again. Jay had ignited some deep-seated hunger that apparently only he could fill. She didn't know what was happening, but she knew it was too late to turn back now.

Chapter 11

Nicole slept like the dead, not regaining consciousness until the sun had come up and cast a warm glow across her bed through the slats of her blinds. Not one for regrets, she wouldn't change a thing about what happened with Jay, she just didn't know how to proceed. She was just getting to the place where she enjoyed Jay's friendship and didn't want to ruin it. She let out a deep sigh, dreading any impending drama.

Jay glanced over at her. "What could possibly be wrong?" He was still basking in the afterglow of the best sex of his life, and she was huffing and puffing.

"Nothing." Nicole looked back at him with a small smile. Trying to avert his questioning.

"A sigh like that doesn't mean 'nothing'." He imitated her fake nice voice, and she rolled her eyes. "I just don't want this to become a big deal. That's all."

Jay glared at her like she was stuck on stupid. "Not a big deal? You damn right this is a big deal. What's your problem?"

"I don't have a problem." She propped up on one elbow. "I just don't need you to go bragging to the world what we did."

"Bragging to the world?" He pointed to himself in confusion. "What am I? A ten-year-old? Why can't you just talk to me instead of always assuming the worst?"

Jay caught himself before he got worked up. He knew Nicole was going to be difficult, it was just her nature, but he was tired of her putting him down at every turn.

"I wasn't assuming," she started, pausing to stare up at him as he got out of bed. Seeing his naked body was doing something to her. "I just know how you used to be with the girls at FAM. We knew everything that went down."

"I think the real question is, why are you comparing yourself to the random chicks I used to smash when I was damn near a teenager?"

He grabbed his pants off the floor and went into the bathroom, closing the door behind him. Nicole blew out a frustrated breath and fell back against her pillow. She hadn't meant to offend him, and knew he had a point. She just didn't know if she was ready for what he claimed he wanted from her, but she also wasn't signing up to be one of his groupies either. Still, Jay had never treated her as such, and she felt bad for upsetting him.

She crawled out of bed, thankful that he wasn't in the room to witness her struggle to use her legs again and pulled on her robe. When he returned, she walked up to him, his shirt in hand.

"I'm sorry. I shouldn't have compared this situation to our college days." He took the shirt and pulled it over his head.

"Is it crazy that your apology is somehow turning me on?" Not one to hold grudges, Jay was pleasantly surprised by her apology and accepted it, knowing how hard it was for her.

"Crazy, but not a surprise." She rolled her eyes but chuckled anyway.

"I'm not playing you, Nicole. Whatever happens between us, I'll always be upfront with you. Can you believe that?"

"I want to," she whispered as she looked up at him to gauge his sincerity.

"So, what's stopping you?" He cocked his head to the side, awaiting her reply.

"You know what?" She looked him over, realizing she was still projecting on him. "Nothing. I believe you. I believe you, and I'm sorry for insinuating that you weren't trustworthy. You're not the one who let me down." She alluded to her soon to be ex-husband.

"I'm not," he confirmed. "And I won't. If you would relax and give me a chance."

"Date if I want, but fuck you," she reiterated his offer.

"That's the plan."

Letting out a long breath she gave him a sly smile.

"I guess we have a deal."

Jay sighed, pulling her into his arms. He lightly brushed a few stray strands of hair out of her face and caressed her cheek with his thumb. She was so damn beautiful, he hated that she wasn't secure enough to trust herself because of whatever went on in her relationship. He would just have to show her he was serious. Then he kissed her, slow and gentle compared to the way he had devoured her earlier. When he pulled away, her eyes were still closed as she recovered from his kiss. "You good?" He asked.

"Mmhmm," she hummed.

"What are your plans for today?"

"Well," she said as she glanced at her bedside clock. "Damn it's after 9:00 a.m. I'm expecting a few deliveries of equipment to finish setting up my office, but other than that, I don't have any other plans."

"What kind of equipment?"

"Let's see. My new PC with accessories, and I

ordered another desk for my projects. Oh, and some shelves for my camera. I'm thinking about getting into photography. If I can write my articles and take the photos, that's more money for me."

Jay nodded. "I can stop by later to help out."

"I think I got it covered, but I'll let you know," she replied. Deciding not to argue with her, he gave her another kiss before letting himself out.

Nicole listened for the front door to close and then fell back onto her bed and squealed. She still couldn't believe what had transpired with Jay. Stretching her hands above her head, she languished in the deliciously sore feeling in between her thighs. It had been too long since she'd been touched, but Trey had never made her body respond the way Jay had. Closing her eyes, she smiled as she remembered the look in his eyes when she first slid down his dick.

Her phone buzzing on the nightstand pulled her out of her thoughts. Sighing, she reached over and checked the caller id. It was Jay.

"Yes?"

"You thinking about it?" He asked.

She grinned. "Maybe."

"Don't lie." His deep voice making her melt.

"Are you?" She asked in return.

"I don't think I'll be able to think of anything else

today."

"Promise?" She teased.

"Promise," he said before ending the call.

"Oh my God," she sighed, Jay's call leaving her tingling. The phone buzzed again in her palm with a call from Kiko.

"Hello?"

"It happened! I know it happened," Kiko shouted on the other line.

"Girl, what are you talking about?" Nicole tried to deflect.

"Don't 'girl' me. I can tell by your sleepy sex voice. He musta had ya ass hollering!"

"Kiko..."

"Yes? Bitch, gets ta talkin'"

"I'm not getting into details, but yes. It did happen and it was good."

"Good? If you don't give me a damn break!"

"Ok. Amazing," Nicole gushed.

"Um, why do you sound so calm and deranged right now? Do I need to come over there?"

"Please! And bring sustenance."

"*I* is on the way," Kiko drawled and hung up.

Nicole slid off the bed and hobbled into the bathroom. A long hot shower was calling her name. She examined herself in the mirror until the steam overtook her reflection. Somehow she thought she would look as different as she felt, but all she found was a hickey on her breast near her nipple. Stepping under the heated burst of water, she moaned in relief. Her back and thigh muscles thanked her.

Visions of the night before flashed behind her lids. Of Jay crooning encouragement as she rode him. Of Jay's expression when he first slid inside her. The way he flipped her on her back and made her come harder than she ever had. All this time she had been worried about him, but now she was concerned that it was her who would become obsessed.

After her shower, Nicole pulled on a comfy pair of FAMU sweats and put her hair into a high bun. Another thing she needed to accomplish was finding a reliable hairdresser. She wouldn't be going to Kiko's girl who charged NFL wife prices, but she needed someone who could make a weave look like it was growing right out of her scalp. While her own hair was thick and hung past her shoulders, she preferred to rock a lace front wig or long micro-braids.

Just as she was walking out of her bedroom, the doorbell rang. Nicole peeped Kiko's red BMW 3 series convertible parked in her driveway.

"You got here quick," she said as she opened the door. Kiko walked in presenting a carrier with bags of fresh takeout.

"And I've come with provisions. Croissant breakfast sandwiches with fries on the side, fresh guac and tortilla chips, and ingredients for our mimosas!" Kiko strolled behind Nicole into the kitchen where she placed everything on the counter. Then, hands on her hips, she turned to face her.

"You know today is a workday. Might have to go easy on the drinks," Nicole noted.

"Girl. What's the point of working for ourselves if we have to follow rules?"

"Without rules, we wouldn't get shit done," Nicole chuckled.

"Good point but go ahead and take it from the top."

Nicole wrinkled her nose, choosing to focus on procuring her breakfast instead of her friend's demand for information. "The top?"

Kiko huffed. "Yes. The top. Meaning, start from the part where you were on a date with Vance and that evolved into you getting wasted with Jay. You guys tried to explain last night, but I'd like a more sober recap."

"Oh, I see," Nicole tittered as she nibbled on a fry. "Well, I'm running on fumes, so I'm gonna take my food into the living room as I process your request."

"I'll take all this food and leave. Don't play with me," Kiko threatened.

"Ok! But I'll be eating and talking cause I'm legit starving."

"Damn. I can tell by the way you're moving, that man put it on you," Kiko said, over enunciating the last few words of her statement.

Nicole's shoulder sagged as she gave up trying to hold it together. "You have no idea. I feel like I need to exchange my thigh joints."

"Just your thighs?" Kiko laughed.

"Had me feeling like a born-again virgin," Nicole replied, causing Kiko to crack up.

"So, I guess the rumors are true," Kiko cackled. Nicole rolled her eyes and shrugged as she pulled out two champagne flutes for their drinks.

"Since he's my boy, I don't need the nitty gritty deets, but I do wanna know how he compares to Trey."

Nicole looked off to the side as she contemplated how to answer that question. It's not like she had a ton of people to compare him to, but she instinctively knew that what Jay had put down on her wasn't even close to typical sex play.

"You know how at Thanksgiving the adults have a table and the kids have their own?"

"Yeah?"

"Well Jay has his own table where he's getting first dibs."

"Wow," Kiko laughed. "Dude got his own table."

"I felt like I didn't want him to stop. Like if we didn't have things to do today we'd still be at it."

"Damn, it's like that?" Kiko raised her brows. "Sounds like someone's sprung."

"I'm not sprung," Nicole denied. "It's been a while for me, and it's different from what I'm used to.

That's all."

"Nicole?"

"Yes?"

"Shut the hell up!"

"What? Why do you say that?"

"Because you've been downplaying this thing with Jay every step of the way. You just said you didn't want the man to stop and in the same breath have the nerve to say it's because 'it's been a while for you' as if there's something wrong with you wanting Jay."

"I didn't say there was anything wrong with it."

"So then just admit it. Stop trying to reason it away. That man has wanted you for years. It's no surprise that he hit you with that presidential treatment."

Nicole rubbed her forehead. "Honestly? I don't know how to feel. I never had these giddy feelings before. Not even with Trey. Don't get me wrong, he put it down in the bedroom, but what I experienced last night was different."

"Oh my gosh, look at your face! Giddy? I think you and Jay may just have something special," Kiko replied.

"Let's not rush to any conclusions. For all I know, he won't even call. Maybe he got what he wanted and won't bother me anymore."

It was Kiko's turn to roll her eyes. "I don't even think you believe that."

"It's a possibility," Nicole said.

"It's silly and you know it."

Nicole sighed. "You're probably right. He got upset when I mentioned how he used to be in college. Asked me why I'm even comparing myself to those chicks."

"And why are you comparing yourself to anyone? Listen, I know you've been going through a lot, and this is new territory for you, but please don't let the past ruin the now. Jay isn't Trey, and you're not some chick sweating him after a game. You're both grown, and I'm sure he's told you what he wants, and if he hasn't he will soon."

"You're right," Nicole grumbled. "It's just crazy that it's happening. Whatever it is."

"Just be honest with him about how you feel, and for God's sake, enjoy yourself!"

Just as Nicole had warned, they spent most of the day drinking and reminiscing. For the first time, she really opened up to Kiko about how hard it was to leave Trey, and how she still missed him sometimes. How hard it was for her to accept that he wasn't who she thought he was. How lonely she felt at times, and how she was afraid that she would get attached to Jay because of her loneliness.

That display of vulnerability led to Kiko revealing that it wasn't all marital bliss between her and Dom. That it was difficult being apart from him for so long, and the fights they had over him making decisions without her input. The latest being a motorcycle that had been delivered to the house. Kiko had no idea that Dom was even into bikes, much less that he had purchased one. She also revealed that even in college they hadn't seen eye to eye on him making decisions that affected them both, and she hoped he would eventually grow out of it.

While Nicole was tidying up the mess her and Kiko had made and attempting to put some of her studio together, she reflected on the last thing her friend had said before she went home.

"I know you're scared, but you're smart enough to know whether whatever you're feeling for Jay is real, or just an itch to be scratched. Don't let your doubts get the best of you."

At the moment, that itch for Jay was raging as she recalled their escapade. She still couldn't believe that he could make her feel so magical. Almost like a literal out of body experience. The more she thought about it, the more she realized that Jay had always been in her peripheral vision. There were times when he'd given her a shoulder to cry on, when he happened to be at the right place at the right time.

Famu Senior Year 2005

"I'm about to pee on myself." Nicole hurried up the driveway to the house they were renting, glad that no one was home if she were not able to make it to the bathroom. Chelle was at work, and Joey was on a date. Shoving her key into the lock, she breathed a sigh of relief when it didn't stick as it did from time to time. Once inside, she threw down her bags, kicked off her heels, and made a beeline to the guest bathroom in the hallway. Not even thinking twice, she threw the door open and ran right into a very naked Jay who was drying his hair with a towel. Nicole threw her hands over her face and screamed just as her eyes caught a glimpse of his thickly hanging third leg. "Oh my God! Get out!"

She could feel the warm flow trickling out as she shoved him out the door and rushed to the toilet.

"What the fuck," she muttered, unable to get the glorious vision of his naked body out of her head. "My clothes are in there," he yelled from the other side of the door.
"Just give me a minute," she hollered back. Shaking her head, she took a few moments, gathered herself and opened the door.

Jay was waiting, towel wrapped around his waist, with a knowing smirk. "You know, I have more interesting ways to make you scream."
"Please shut the fuck up and put your clothes on," she grumbled.
"I'm the one who should be upset. You barged in on me."
"Well, I'm the one who actually lives here. The

house was supposed to be empty. Why the hell are you here?"

"I always hang out here if Shane has company. You're usually in the room with your hubby," Jay said matter-of-factly. "Where's he at this weekend?"

"None of your business."

Nicole knew it was a topic of conversation that Trey was gone more and more since moving down from New York. She'd gotten the house so that they could spend more time together, but he was spending most of his time down in Miami 'working' with his cousin.

Jay shrugged and went back into the bathroom to get dressed. Nicole grabbed her things and headed to her own room to shower and change. She had the master suite with its own bathroom. When she was done, she pulled on a pair of sweats and headed for the kitchen. Jay was lounging on the couch watching a movie and munching on popcorn. Grabbing a glass of wine as she had intended, she joined him, sitting on the couch with her legs tucked underneath her.

"Have your eyes recovered yet?"

"If you mention it again, I'm kicking you out. Chelle and Joey aren't here to advocate for you. Now, what are you watching?"

"*Boomerang.* Kiko swears it's a classic, but I've

never seen it," he replied.

"What? Oh, you have to watch it. It's one of my favorites."

"Is it ok if we turn off the lights? I don't want you to be scared or anything."

"Why would I be scared?"

Jay shrugged. "I don't know. Just making sure."

It took her a minute, but she realized he was referring to her screaming at the sight of him.

"For the record, I was surprised. Not scared!"

Jay laughed. "But why you covered your eyes like that?"

"I'm a married woman, in case you forgot. I don't need to know what your junk looks like."

"But–"

"If you say something slick, I swear to God you're out of here," she threatened.

"Ok," he chuckled. "Turn the lamp off and pass the wine."

They watched the movie in comfortable silence peppered with a few laughs until they got to the part of where the male lead pulls back the blankets to look at the female lead's feet. Jay laughed and Nicole shook her head.

"Is it really that serious?"

"Yes," Jay chuckled.

 "What if she was a dancer and that jacked up her toes?"

Jay gave her a doubtful look and then glanced down at her feet which were still tucked away.

"Oh no you don't," she cried as he lunged forward and grabbed her leg.

"Let me see yours," he demanded.

"No," Nicole laughed, trying to get away from him to no avail. Jay all but dragged her until he was able to access her feet.

"Oh," he said. "You have pretty feet. I thought you were talkin' bout yourself."

"Whatever," she huffed and attempted to pull her foot back.

"Hold up. Your feet are pretty and soft," he said as he began to massage her heel. As much as Nicole wanted to pull away, it felt too incredible to stop.

"Ugh," she moaned.

"Damn," Jay murmured. "You don't get many foot rubs, do you?"

Nicole gave him the side eye before answering, "No."

"What? I'd be rubbing you down every night if I had the chance. Trey is trippin'."

"Yeah well, he ain't here so less talking and more rubbing."

"Where is he, anyways?"

She released a long sigh. "In Miami, working."

Jay's lips formed a tight line, but he didn't say anything. He'd noticed how often Trey was away, and heard the grumblings from the girls, who were concerned for their friend. They were having a good time together, and he didn't want to mess it up by telling her that her husband was a piece of shit. As he rubbed her foot, he slowly inched upwards until he was eventually massaging her calf muscles. Nicole's eyes were closed, and her body was relaxed. He wanted so badly to pull her into his arms.

"Why did you ask me that and then get quiet," she asked. Eyes still closed.
"Because. That's your relationship. It's not my place to judge anything about it. Unless you ask my opinion, I'm keeping it to myself."

Nicole's eyes drifted open and she regarded him for a moment before she asked him to elaborate.

"I don't know, Nick. You're smart, fuckin' beautiful, like stare at your face all day beautiful, and your body is," he trailed off as he looked her over for emphasis.
"Ok, so what are you saying?"
"I'm saying that if I were your man I'd be all up on you and no other man would have the chance to even come near your pretty ass feet."

That statement made her feel a bit self-conscious and she realized his hands had moved away from her feet a while ago. Giving him a sheepish smile, she slowly pulled her feet back to her safe zone.

"I'm not stupid, you know. Everyone thinks I don't see what he's up to, but the truth is I don't know what to do. My parents won't get involved because they said if I was grown enough to run off and get married, then I'm grown enough to deal with my situation. I know he loves me, but I don't feel like a wife. I thought us finally living together would help things, but he just found another way to put distance between us. I love Trey, but sometimes I feel trapped."

Jay looked away from her and shook his head. It angered him to think that anyone could treat her that way, and the sadness in her eyes was tempting him to make her feel better, if only for a little while. If there was one thing he was good at, besides basketball, it was reading women, and he knew that if he wanted to, he could have Nicole on her back in minutes. But he cared about her too much to do that to her.

"I think you should let go of the whole idea of what being married is supposed to feel like. Focus on graduating and set a plan for yourself. You're too young to settle into a relationship just because you rushed into something when you were eighteen. And you never have to feel trapped because I'll always have your back."

"Thanks, Jay," she sniffed as she swiped a tear from the corner of her eyes. It was the best advice she'd gotten regarding her relationship, and for once, she felt like there was a light at the end of the tunnel.

Chapter 12

Nicole was half-heartedly setting up her new equipment when her phone buzzed.

`Jay: Open the door`

She checked her phone for missed calls or messages, but there weren't any. While she knew he said he would help her, she didn't expect him to just pop up. Still, she smoothed her bun and popped a couple of Altoids in her mouth before answering the door. Jay was standing there looking good as hell in gray joggers and a crisp white t-shirt that clung to his muscular frame. He held up two bags of takeout.

"I hope you haven't eaten yet," he said as he walked in the door.

"You would know the answer if you had called

first," she sassed.

"Behave, or you won't get your surprise." He bumped her from behind as he guided her toward her dining room table. Before she could inspect what was in the bags, he pounced.

"I've been thinking 'bout your ass all day," he murmured as he grasped each voluptuous cheek and pulled her against him. "And you smell so fuckin' good."

He shoved his face into her neck, inhaling deeply before he began to kiss her sensitive skin. Nicole's hands explored him all over, just as excited to be in his arms again. When he bit her ear lobe she whimpered. Somehow, he made the sting feel good by sucking it. He picked her up off her feet and moved to the side of the table that was empty and laid her on her back.

"What are you doing?" She groaned, as he slid his hand between her thighs.

"I need a little appetizer," he replied with a mischievous grin.

Pulling her forward until her legs were hanging off the table, he spread her open. Leaning over her, he kissed her gently as his hand slipped inside her pants. He sucked her bottom lip while he teased her clit. Nicole arched into his touch, sighing in pleasure.

Jay grabbed the waistband of her sweats and

yanked them off in one aggressive tug. His eyes never left hers as he freed his erection from his own pants, stroking himself a few times before tapping it against her clit. He teased her mercilessly, gliding the head of his shaft across her sensitive nub. First back and forth, and then in a circle. Over and over until she was begging him to put it in.

"I told you I wanted an appetizer," he said as he crouched down and slurped and sucked her aching rigid peak. Nicole was so high strung she came almost as soon as his mouth touched her.

"Shit, Jay! I'm coming," she cried out.

Just when she thought the torture was over, he stopped, stood up, grabbed her thighs, and plunged into her. Nicole screamed in ecstasy as her orgasm rippled from the pressure of his dick inside her mixed with the slight soreness from the night before. Her pussy had been swollen and sensitive all day, and the feel of him was exquisite. He deep stroked her through her climax, staring at where their bodies came together like he'd never seen anything like it in his life. Mesmerized.

"You got some type of magic in this little pussy, I swear," he groaned as he slid his shaft in and out. "I love the way you take my dick."
"Oh, God," she moaned in response. Nicole began to work her hips, already feeling another climax

building. The intense pleasure of his slow pace drove her crazy. Jay thumbed her clit again, keeping his stroke steady.

"I feel you, baby. Squeezing me," he uttered. "You bout to come again. Come on Nicky. Come all over my dick."

"Ahh," Nicole cried out as she came apart. Jay's sexy vocal encouragement was enough to push her over the edge. Again. It felt like some sort of vortex of pleasure was swirling and swirling in her core. She thrust her hips upwards, increasing the pressure of his thumb. She moaned loudly when he grasped her hips and began to pump harder.

"Look at me," he growled. "Look at how hard you're gonna make me come."

Nicole did as she was told, watching as the beautiful man above her clenched his chiseled jaw, slowly closed his eyes, and let his head hang back as his dick jerked inside of her. His tortured moans aroused her even more and her pussy clenched around him even harder.

"Shit," he groaned as his load shot inside of her. He reached for her, pulling her into his arms and stunning her with a wild and passionate kiss. It was a sweet contrast to how physical he'd just been with her. Nicole threw her arms around his neck, holding on for dear life. Jay was a force to be reckoned with, and she loved thinking of all the ways she would have to keep up.

After a hot shower, mostly spent with Jay fucking her up against the tiled wall, they sat wrapped up in towels eating sushi from Zuma.

"I can't believe how good this is," she gushed while nibbling a piece of sashimi.
"Wait till things die down a bit. I'll take you there so you can try the king crab and a few other items on the menu I know you'll like."
"Yum, I can't wait."
"Greedy as ever," he teased.
"Whatever," she chuckled. Then, remembering something from the night before, she turned serious. "Vance mentioned something about how your team did you. What's that about?"
"Damn. He was in my business like that?" Jay wiped his hands with a napkin and sipped his drink before answering. "Well, when I injured my knee the first doctor said I would be out for two seasons, but I got a second opinion that said one season max with rigorous rehab. The Heat cut me based on the first doctor. I got paid a good chunk of my contract, thanks to Chelle, but it hurt my career in the NBA."
"Wow. That's messed up. How's your knee now?"
"I'm fit enough to play and been invited to try out with a couple of teams. I also have interest from France and Italy's Euro league teams."
"So do you want to play here or abroad?"
Hearing him talk about possibly moving away

made Nicole feel like she was eating bricks and not sushi.

"I don't know. Just weighing my options right now. The money will be better here, but the experience will be more exciting in Europe. Or, I could do neither and focus on building my empire."

He said, watching Nicole to gauge her response. Her face remained passive, for the most part, except for a twitch of her lips. He'd noticed her little frown when he mentioned Europe.

"Wow. Europe would be dope," she said in a faraway voice. "I've always wanted to visit Milan and Paris. What do you want to do?"

"Honestly? I'm not sure. My dream growing up was to play in the NBA, but now I'm not so sure. I think seeing the world and meeting new people would be cool, or playing for another city in the states. Maybe I'm outgrowing Miami. We'll see."

"You mean move and not be a part of the South Beach mix anymore?" She replied, voice laced with sarcasm. Jay laughed.

"I still can't get over your date," he said using air quotes.

"I'm trying to forget it." She rolled her eyes.

Jay laughed. "Ok. I'll try not to bring it up again."

"Thank you," she smirked. "I guess it'll make a cute story for my grandkids someday."

"You mean our grandkids," he corrected her, wiggling his brows.

"Oh, stop." She nudged his shoulder playfully.

"You think I'm playing with you," he said.

"I don't really know what to think to be honest, but I *know* that for the time being I'm still married and not in the market to swap out husbands. Jay smirked. "Ok."

Nicole narrowed her eyes at him. "Why did you say it like that? I'm serious, Jay. I told you that I want to date other people."

"And I told you to date other people but fuck me. What's the issue?"

"The issue is that you sound mad possessive."

Jay didn't respond. He took a sip of his wine, his eyes fixed on Nicole's, and put his glass on the end table. She watched in confusion as he moved everything out the way and knelt toward her.

"What are you about to do?" Her voice betrayed her with a slight tremble. The look in his eyes told her exactly what he was about to do, but she couldn't believe that he had it in him, or that her body wanted him to do it. With just a look.

"Behave," she said weakly as he pushed her back to the ground and hovered over her.

"You tell me to behave, but spread your legs wide open for me," he grinned. He whipped his towel away and pulled hers open. "You said I'm possessive, huh?"

This time there wasn't any teasing or torture. Jay thrust into her in one smooth motion, still looking into her eyes.

"Does this feel possessive? Hmm?"

Bending forward, his tongue traced the seam of her lips, his kiss soft in contrast to his rough strokes.

"Because you possessed me the second you slid your sweet pussy down my dick. You think it's gonna feel like this with anyone else? Huh? You think Vance could make you feel like this?" He punctuated each question with a hard thrust.
"Jay!"
"Answer me." He rode her hard and she screamed his name again. "You want someone else?"
"No," she whimpered. "No one else." She placed her hands on his shoulders, her nails digging into his flesh. Her eyes rolled back as every sensor in her body lit up like a Christmas tree. She didn't know what Jay had done to her, but she couldn't even think of anyone else touching her.

"You want me to give this dick to someone else?" He whispered, his mouth brushing hers.
"No!" The thought pissed her off and she bit his lip. Jay laughed.
"You sound a lil possessive, Nicky," he said as he began a slow, torturous pace.
"Shut up," she gasped.

Her pussy quivered around his shaft when he hit her spot. Noticing her reaction, he repeated the motion over and over until she was moaning his name.

"You love me, Nicky?"

"Jay," she barely managed. Her mind and body were twisted with the way he was handling her.

Pulling out, he turned her around, kneeling her in front of the couch. Nicole placed her hands on the cushion for support as he entered her from behind. One hand grasped her hip as the other roamed her torso, stopping to fondle her breasts and then resting around her throat.

"Mine," he uttered as he punished her from the back. "You don't have to say it back. I know you're mine."

He licked a trail up her back, kissed along the back of her neck, and nipped at her shoulder. Nicole's moans turned to, grunts that turned into her gasping as her body primed for release.

"Oh, shit," she cried out. Her arms went limp, and she slumped forward, her orgasm striking like lightning. Everywhere tingled, and her pussy gushed around his shaft.

"Nicky, Nicky, Nicky," Jay moaned as he followed her into their shared ecstasy.

When they finally made it to the bedroom, Jay curled around Nicole's body as they got comfortable in bed. That seemed like the only place they hadn't had sex that night. His kiss was gentle and soft, and there weren't any sexual advances. Nicole felt a swell of emotion in her chest that threatened to bring her to tears. She didn't understand why she felt that way.

"Jay," she whispered, pulling away to catch her breath.

"What's wrong?"

"Nothing's wrong. I just," she paused, not sure what she was trying to say. "When I said I wanted to date earlier, it wasn't because I don't want you. I just want to know what freedom feels like."

"Are you doing anything you don't want to do?"

"No."

"And I won't ever ask or force you to," he said.

"Yeah, but I can't say no to you," she replied.

"You don't want to say no to me," he grinned. "Don't stress yourself out. It'll make sense to you, eventually."

She chuckled. "What does that mean?"

"Give me a kiss goodnight and go to sleep. I'll put your office together in the morning before I hit the gym."

She returned the sweet kiss he had given her before. "I'm happy you're here."

He kissed her forehead and sighed. "I know."

∞∞∞

"Houston, we have a problem," Nicole said to Chelle via Facetime.

"Uh oh. This is serious," Chelle replied.
"Where's Remy?"
"He's at the dealership. Why? What's going on?"
"I think I have feelings for Jay."
"Next thing you'll be telling me who invented the theory of relativity," Chelle joked.
"Be serious! I mean *feelings*!"
"What kind of *feelings*, Nicole? Use your words!"
"He got me to admit that I don't want anyone else, and while he was kissing me, just kissing no sex, I almost started crying. What the fuck is wrong with me?"

Chelle sat up in her bed and stared at Nicole through the small rectangle on the screen.

"Whoa."
"Whoa? That's all you got? I called you because you're the logical one. I'm expecting more than whoa. Use *your* words!"
"I said whoa because I didn't want to blurt out that you love him," Chelle shouted.
"*Love*?" Nicole echoed and fell back onto her own

pillows. "Is that what this is? *Or*, is he just fucking the sense out of me?"

"Well, if that's the case, you wouldn't feel shit as soon as he was done. Your ass wanted to cry because he was kissing you."

"And I told him I was happy he was here with me. His cocky ass gonna say 'I know' in a smug tone."

"Maybe if you would listen, with your hard-headed ass, you would have heard when I told you that Jay has wanted you for a long time. And if I'm being honest, I think you've liked Jay for a long time, and now those feelings can finally find a home."

"I think chalking it up to the sex is much easier," Nicole sighed.

"Well, it's a small probability. If you hadn't known the fool for almost ten years, I might say yeah, it's the sex, but..."

"But? But what?"

"From everything you've been telling me, it's been kinda building up to this. Or he's gotten through your armor. But fuck all this speculating. Just tell me what you're feeling."

"I don't know how to describe it. Like when he popped up here last night, I wanted to be annoyed but I was totally excited. And when I saw that he brought food? I was elated."

"Greedy," Chelle teased.

"But seriously. My favorite part is cuddling. And I love how he just does what needs to be done. He knew I had to put my office together and he got up early this morning and did it before he left. It's like part of me thinks I need my space and freedom and the other part wants him all up in my space. Like if he doesn't come over tonight, I'm going to be disappointed," Nicole explained.

"So, tell me more about you admitting that you're his?"

"Oh, gawd," Nicole groaned. "Why did I mention that?"

Chelle laughed. "Let me guess. He was balls deep when this admission occurred?"

"And here I was worried about him blabbing my business. I'm no damn better!"

"Well, you know I'm not gonna tell anyone. Not even Remy. Besides, Jay would not put you out there like that. Whenever Remy asks about you, he just smiles and says you're good."

"He smiles?" Nicole swooned.

"Yes. Dimples popping and all that."

"How did I have him pegged so wrong?"

"Cause. That was the only way to ensure that nothing happened. You two have always had chemistry, but anytime you started having too much fun with him, you turned mean. Self-preservation, if you will."

"I guess. Chelle, I've never felt like this," she said in a more sober tone.

"I know, babe. And I'm so happy for you. Jay's a good guy, and a millionaire. You could do worse."

"Excuse me? A what-a-naire?"

"You heard what I said. He got a good portion

of his contract, and he's made great investments. As a matter of fact, I think a few teams overseas have offered him contracts, and even a couple of NBA teams have invited him to tryouts. Jay has options. So, keep that in mind when your mean streak tries to rear its ugly head."

That warning would haunt Nicole for the rest of the day. She was getting dressed to meet Mallory and Kiko at club Liv. Their plan was to party that night, spend the night at Kiko's since Dom was playing an away game, and then do their weekly brunch the next day. Nicole was looking forward to her first real night of clubbing as a single woman. She didn't know why she was so enamored with the title, especially when everyone else was racing to get hitched. It was her independence from her husband that she valued above anything, and all that it entailed.

The weather was cooling down as fall came into full effect, and while it was still much warmer than what she was used to in NYC, it wasn't exactly summer temperatures. She had her shoes picked out, but sifted through her closet for the right outfit, deciding on a black, long-sleeved bodysuit that had a zipper that ran down her back to the crack of her ass. Her lace front was styled into a sleek side-part ponytail, and gold accessories adorned her ears and neck.

"Damn, I look good," she mused as she regarded

herself in the mirror.

Grabbing her phone, overnight bag, wallet, and keys, she stuffed them into her red Celine trio crossbody bag. Kiko had their personal driver pick her up since she was the furthest away from the club. It made no sense for her to drive since she would be drinking, and they were all going back to Kiko's together. She slid into the black sedan and texted her girls that she was on her way.

They were awaiting her arrival outside the notorious hotspot, Kiko in a gunmetal top, jeans, and suede booties that coordinated with her Louis Vuitton Twist purse, and Mallory in a black lace bodysuit, short denim skirt and silver stilettos. Nicole recognized a few of the girls that had joined them for drinks when she was out with Jay. Collectively, they all looked like they stepped out of a music video. Kiko nodded to the bouncer, and they were all allowed entry without question, and led to a VIP section by the host.

"It's good to have friends in high places, "Nicole snickered to Mallory, who nodded in agreement. "You know Dom is a hometown hero. They get treated like royalty wherever they go."
"I see!"
"Jay, too," Mallory slid in.

Nicole just gave her the side-eye but didn't even

bother protesting. At some point, she would have to concede that Kiko and Mal were right about him, and her possible feelings for him. It was still surreal to her that not only did they hook up, but that she hadn't been able to stop thinking about him, and she was sure that he felt the same way.

"What are you smiling about?" Kiko nudged her shoulder bringing her back to the present.
"Nothing. Just excited to be out and ready to have some fun tonight."
"Good answer," Kiko smirked, but she didn't push the subject. "I was thinking about what to do for your birthday."
"Hmm," Nicole considered her suggestion. "I was thinking. How about we rent a big house instead of staying in a hotel?"
"That's exactly what I was thinking. Maybe even throw a little after party after the Alumni event.

Halloween had always been a special occasion for the crew because it was also Nicole's birthday. If they didn't throw their own party, they usually attended a costume party to celebrate. Now that they were older and mostly coupled up, it made more sense to rent a house and throw an intimate party than going to a club. It also happened to be FAMU Homecoming, and there was an alumni event so they could make a weekend of it.

"Oooh! I like that idea. And I won't have to worry about too much. Since Joey, Chelle, and Remy are coming down, it would be cool for us all to stay in the same place."

Nicole frowned. "What about Shane?"

"Depending on where his game is that week, he said he'll try to join. Honestly? I think he's waiting to find out if Joey is coming with Dante."

"Ah," Nicole replied. "They are still going strong. I'm proud of our girl."

"Yeah. Joey in a relationship is mind blowing, but we are all growing up," Kiko sighed wistfully.

"But isn't Shane dating some girl he went to high school with? What does he care about Dante for?"

"Your nosey ass knows better than me. I'm just speculating," Kiko chuckled. "You know who would know?"

"Chelle!" They both said at the same time.

The bottle girl came with their drinks and after they were all set up with a glass, Kiko said a cute toast encouraging new beginnings and having a blast. Nicole received both messages and did just that, getting right out on the dance floor. Just like their school days, Kiko and Nicole fed off each other's energy. They danced together and apart; matching each other's movements when a certain song came on that they had a routine too. Mallory found a dance partner and was grinding on him for most of the night.

"I don't know about you, but I'm starving," Kiko said as they piled into the car that would take them back to her apartment.

"I could definitely eat," Mal agreed.

"I need a foot rub," Nicole groaned. "Cute heels and dancing all night do not go hand in hand."

"Hmm," Kiko hummed. "I know someone who could help you out with that."

"Hush!" Nicole put a finger over her lips to silence her friend.

"I'm just saying," Kiko mumbled around her finger.

"We are having girls' night. We should stop and get cheeseburgers or something." Nicole attempted to change the subject.

"Girl! If you don't text that man and get your foot rub," Mal called out.

"It's late," Nicole protested.

"I know you're new to this, but it's called a booty call. Just call him."

Nicole glared at both women but dug in her bag for her phone. Secretly, she wanted to see Jay but didn't want to bail on their girls' night plans. He answered on the second ring, his deep voice reverberating from her speaker.

"Come over," he said without any greeting or fanfare.

"Hello to you too," Nicole replied.

"Hello. It's 3:00 am and you woke me up, so come put me back to sleep."

He hung up, and Nicole glanced up to find Kiko

and Mal both looking at her expectantly. She realized she was biting her lip, and grinned. "Hey guys. I'm going to Jay's."

"We heard," Kiko said.

"Yes. His instructions were quite clear," Mal added.

They arrived at Kiko's building after stopping for food, and Nicole hugged both of her friends before heading toward the elevator bank to Jay's building. As she strolled through the lobby her anticipation of seeing him increased. It hit her just how bad she wanted him as the wetness pooled in her panties.

When she stepped off the elevator, she locked eyes with Jay, who was leaning in his doorway waiting for her. She stepped gingerly on her aching feet but maintained her sexy strut. He watched her with a hunger in his eyes that caused her core to tremble. When she got close enough, he pulled her against him.

"Did you know I've been craving you all day?"

"Craving?" Nicole simpered up at him, running a hand down his bare chest.

"Craving," he repeated.

Jay reached behind her, pulling her zipper all the way down, and pushed his hand inside, gripping an ass cheek before sliding two fingers into her wetness. Nicole moaned softly, eyes still on his as she hiked her leg up around his waist for better access. He brought his hand to his lips and sucked her essence off his fingers like it was honey, the sight causing a level five tidal wave between her thighs. She pulled his head down and sealed her lips to his.

Jay swept her off her feet, carrying her into his bedroom so he could show her just how much he had been craving her.

Chapter 13

"I think we should go for a simple and clean theme for the website," Nicole said to Kiko as they collaborated with Gerrard, their web developer.

Being able to work with each other in person proved to be fruitful, and the duo was able to create and implement a plan to transition their fashion blog to a website and YouTube channel. They started with bimonthly topics with quick snippets to promote the longer content and the blog posts. It had been such a success with Kiko's following that they moved ahead with their plans to expand. Dom bought a storefront that Jay had found for them to work out of.

"I trust your eye. Let's keep the colors pink, white, black, and gold, and base our new logo around that," Kiko added.

"Sounds good," Gerrard concluded.

He flashed Nicole a dazzling smile as he packed up his laptop and equipment, which she returned with a curt nod. Kiko patted his shoulder, partly in thanks, partly in consolation. He'd been trying unsuccessfully to flirt with Nicole since they started working with him. After he walked out of their studio, Kiko turned to her friend.

"Do we need to get you some glasses?"
Nicole looked up from her computer. "Huh?"
"Cause you act like you don't see that man whenever he walks his nerd-fine ass up in here."
"Girl, please," Nicole waved her off. "Gerrard needs to learn to use his words if he's really interested."
"Really? Kiko perched on the edge of the desk. "Maybe he would if you gave him the signal. A lil smile or somethin'."
"Whatever. I don't really want to mix business and pleasure."
"Whatever, for real. Your smitten ass wouldn't go for it even if he boldly invited you out on a date. You know the thing you swore you wanted to do to get your groove back?"
Nicole smirked. "I'm getting my groove back just fine."
"I see you didn't deny being smitten."
Nicole grinned.
"My boy Jay got you up in here blushing. Hold

up." Kiko reached across the desk for her cell phone and video called Chelle.

"Oh, Lord," Nicole groaned. "What are you about to do?"

Chelle's round face came into view with her office as the backdrop. "Waddup!"

"Wassup, boo," Kiko greeted her. "You good for a quick chat?"

After passing the bar exam, Chelle's position in her company increased along with her workload. She was well on her way in her endeavor to be a successful Sports and Entertainment lawyer. She was already handling legal matters for Jay, Shane, and Dom, and helped Nicole and Kiko structure their business. She was usually busy, so they always made sure before launching into their shenanigans.

"I've got time. I'm technically on lunch, but you know how that goes."

"Yeah. I know you're a workaholic. I also know Remy would have a fit if he knew you were skipping lunch."

"Well, once I'm my own boss I'll be able to take lunch when I want, for how long. Now, I heard grumpy smurf in the background. What's going on?"

"I am not grumpy!" Nicole mugged the screen.

"Doesn't seem like it," Chelle teased, blowing Nicole a kiss.

"We might have to change her name, though," Kiko chuckled.

"To what?"

"Smitten Smurf!" Kiko's exaggerated voice had Chelle giggling.

"Excuse me?" Chelle continued to laugh.

"Jay got this girl justa sinnin' and grinnin' as my granny used to say."

"Why are you discussing me like I'm not sitting right here?"

"Well, what do you have to say for yourself?" Chelle asked Nicole.

Before she could answer, a private delivery guy pushed the door to their suite open holding a bouquet of pink and red roses, and a stack of two boxes from Chanel. One medium sized and one large.

"I'm looking for Nicole Montgomery?"

"Montgomery?" Kiko exclaimed. "I *know* he did not."

"What's going on?" Chelle couldn't see anything but Kiko's surprised facial expression.

Nicole got up from her desk, rolled her eyes at Kiko and raised her hand. "Those are for me."

She took the vase and reached into her Prada fanny pack for a tip.

"That won't be necessary, Miss. The sender already took care of me. Have a great day." He placed the boxes on the desk, smiled at both ladies, and sauntered back out the door.

"Hello," Chelle called out.

"Girl," Kiko replied. "It's flowers and something from Chanel!"

"We are on a video call. Let me see what's going on!"

"Oh, sorry." Kiko turned the phone so that Chelle could watch along while Nicole opened the envelope with the note for the flowers. She read the note to herself first, making sure he didn't say anything too crazy.

Congratulations to you and Kiko on accomplishing your first business goal and getting your magazine off the ground. The big one is for you, Love. You deserve it.

"Love?" Kiko snatched the card out of Nicole's hand to read it for herself.

"Open the box," Chelle urged.

"Ok!" Nicole's entire mood changed, and she was bristling with excitement.

"He got us both something? Aww," Kiko gushed.

Nicole carefully pulled the monogramed ribbon that kept the two boxes stacked together loose and placed it to the side, then she handed the smaller one to Kiko who didn't hesitate to open it. Turning to the desk, Nicole's heart raced as she opened her gift. She was used to getting presents, Trey got her gifts all the time, but this was different.

"I can't believe him," she gasped when she recognized the bag he'd given her. Nicole couldn't help but smile as she gazed at the Chanel Logo Calfskin Hobo Shoulder Tote with the thick chain. It was at the top of her wish list, but she'd never told him about it.

"How could he know?"

"What is it? "Chelle was all but yelling at this point.
Kiko paused showing off her gift of a black 2.55 Chanel purse to see what had Nicole stunned, making sure to turn the phone before Chelle barked at her again.

"Ooh, that's nice," Chelle's voice echoed through the speaker, as she smiled like a proud mama. "Jay did good, right Kiko?
"He shole did," Kiko drawled, nodding in agreement. When Nicole furrowed her eyebrow in confusion she added, "Ya boy asked around and we gave him about ten options of what you might like."

"Wow," Nicole uttered, continuing to admire her new bag. She couldn't wait to wear it, knowing that it would pair well with almost anything. That's why she loved it so much. Jay deserved a big thank you, and she couldn't wait to give it to him. To think that a few weeks ago she would have balked at the thought of letting him touch her, now it was almost all she could think of.

Nicole's cheeks hurt from smiling so hard. Jay made her feel seen and demonstrating that he listened to her, and paid attention made her heart flutter. She wasn't ready to admit it out loud, but he had really grown on her, and she found herself looking forward to seeing him. When she had showed up at his apartment for their first booty-call, he told her that he was becoming addicted to sleeping next to her. For all the years she'd been married, there had never been that level of intimacy with her husband.

Still holding her gift, she grabbed her phone off the desk to Facetime him. The phone almost rang out, but he answered at the last second. His handsome face donning clear rimmed glasses as he sat in his home office when he appeared on the screen

"Hey, beautiful."

"Jay," Nicole sighed in satisfaction. "We got your presents. You shouldn't– "

"Should've seen her face when she saw the bag she's been lusting after," Kiko chimed in, cutting her off before she had the chance to downplay the moment. She screwed up her face at Nicole, gesturing for her to 'cut it out.'

"Thank you. I love it," Nicole said with a bigger smile causing Kiko to nod in approval.

"I just love how you got my girl smiling," Chelle

chimed in. "But the bag is dope too!"

"Wassup fam. Thanks for the help," Jay said, mimicking Chelle's New York accent.

"No problem," Chelle replied. "Love you guys, but I've got a meeting with a potential client. See you in a few days." And with that, she was gone.

"Come by tonight and get the rest of your, uh, surprise." He smirked and Nicole picked up on his meaning.

"Oh, there's more?" Nicole eyed him suggestively.

"Maybe," he drawled.

"Promise?"

Jay winked before ending the call.

"Ok. That's the second time I've heard that. You guys already had your own inside jokes?" Kiko folded her arms, eyeing Nicole with curiosity. Not only was it the first time she'd seen her friend this happy, but it was the first time she'd seen that glow of love in her eyes. Nicole and Trey had grown to be distant and tumultuous over the years, leaving Nicole always on edge or irritable.

Nicole grinned. "It's nothing crazy. He started it when I moved down. It's funny to me," she said as her phone vibrated with a text.

```
Jay: Can't wait to taste my pussy
Nicole: Can't wait to thank u
Jay: What u have in mind?
Nicole: It involves swallowing
```

`Jay: I'm hard as a calculus exam`

"Hmm. Funny, you say?" Kiko eyed her sarcastically. "Y'all are nasty, by the way. "

"What?" Nicole gave her an innocent look.

Kiko chuckled. "Oh, nothing. Just taking it all in."

∞∞∞

The plan was for Kiko and Nicole to be the first to arrive at their six-bedroom Airbnb, chartering a short flight from Fort Lauderdale Airport and then driving a rental car to the house. Jay had a tryout with the Dallas Mavericks and would join them later, Chelle and Remy were on a flight from New York, and Joey, Dante and Shane were flying in from the west coast.

When they arrived the house was immaculate, but per Chelle's instructions, they had to do a refresher by wiping down all surfaces. Kiko started that task and sent Nicole to the store to pick up the liquor, and dinner for the evening. Her birthday was the next night, and they'd celebrate after the Alumni mixer.

Nicole found that being back in Tallahassee brought back a lot of fond memories, and she soaked in the buzzing energy of Homecoming weekend. She was on a high when she returned to the house, excited for their friends to arrive.

"Lucy!," she called out. "I'm home!"

"I'm in the kitchen," Kiko called back.

"The kitchen," Nicole murmured to herself. "Now, if I were a kitchen, where would I be?"

She wandered through the lower level of the large house toward where she assumed the kitchen was located. When she entered she almost fainted when everyone shouted out, "Happy birthday!"

Nicole clapped a hand over her mouth in shock. She looked around the room and everyone was there, Chelle and Remy, Jay, Kiko, Joey and Dante, and Shane who was standing with a woman she didn't recognize. The way she had her hazel eyes watching Joey like a hawk, Nicole deduced that must be his new girlfriend. The only person who was missing was Dom, who had an away game in Washington D.C. that weekend.

"I can't believe you guys," she said, voice trembling.

The nostalgia of the weekend and seeing all her friends together again had her feeling emotional. The room was decorated with pink birthday accessories, and a pink and white two-layer cake with a single candle in the center waited for her to blow it out. Looking around the room again, she sighed in happiness, eyes smiling when she met Jay's.

"Make a wish," Joey yelled out.

Stepping forward, Nicole closed her eyes tight for a few seconds before blowing out her candle. Everyone cheered and her girls crowded around her for a group hug.

"We know it's not your birthday until tomorrow, but this was the only way to surprise your nosey ass," Chelle explained.

"I'm not that bad," she whined.

"Um, yes the hell you are," Joey shot back. Taking a dollop of icing and dabbing it on Nicole's nose.

"Joey," Nicole squealed as she swiped at the sugary mess.

"She has a point," Kiko giggled.

Deciding to save the cake for after dinner, they ate from their favorite seafood spot known for its jumbo fried shrimp and seafood gumbo. Then, they debated going out to see what the festivities after the game would be like, but half of the group was up for it, and the other just wanted to chill. Of course, the guys wanted to go, so Remy, Jay, Shane, and his girlfriend, Kelly left. Joey stayed behind with Dante who spent most of the time in the bedroom working, and Nicole and Chelle weren't in the mood to turn up. The four friends sat in the enclosed screened porch, sipping wine, and catching up.

"So," Joey drawled. "Noticed your luggage wound

up in the room with Jay's luggage," she said to Nicole.

"Isn't that interesting," Nicole gasped. "Almost as interesting as the way Kelly keeps giving you the death glare."

"Uh uh," Chelle hummed. "Don't try to distract us with the obvious. We all knew Jay and Nicole were bound to happen. What's going on with you and Shane? You've barely said anything to each other?"

"Jay and Nicole were bound to happen?" Nicole parroted, but Kiko waved her off.

"Yeah, boo. Sorry you were the last to know. But back to Joey. What's the weird vibes?"

Joey sighed, rolling her eyes. "It's so dumb. They're dating long-distance, so shit is already tense, but when he played in LA, we hung out after the game like we always do. I guess he didn't tell Kelly about it, and she says she thinks there's more between us than just friends. She tried to tell him to cut me off, but, duh, I'm his publicist."

The other three girls were quiet, all looking to see who was gonna be the first to speak up.

"Well," Chelle cleared her throat. "Is she wrong?"

"Girl, I'm glad you said it and not me," Nicole drawled.

"I mean, Joey. We've been asking that for years, and we're your friends," Kiko reasoned.

"You know Shane is like –"

"*Jonelle Marie Duval!* If you say like your brother,

I'm gonna throat chop you," Chelle threatened.

"Yeah! Show us some respect," Kiko demanded as she dissolved into giggles over Chelle's threat.

"I'm saying," Nicole chuckled. "I think we've all heard enough of that lie."

"Whatever," Joey said over their laughter. "You didn't have to use my full government! I was going to say my best friend."

"Excuse me?" Chelle squeaked.

"You know what I mean," Joey clarified. "You're my girl, but it's different when you can talk to a guy about anything."

"So why haven't you guys tried to date?" Kiko asked.

"Or have you dated?" Nicole questioned.

"Shane isn't my type and I'm not his. We both want different things, and we respect that about each other," Joey replied, not answering either question, causing a collective groan. When no one spoke up she continued. "Besides, he's enjoying his bad boy era."

"I noticed that," Chelle said. "He has been wilding out lately. I don't know if Kelly is in it for the love or for the money, but she's putting up with a lot."

"Shane?" Kiko was shocked. "I can't imagine it."

"Yup. Between the tattoos, the parties, and the women? He's earning quite the reputation," Joey replied.

"Way to deflect," Chelle grinned.

"That's fine, Joey. Keep your secrets," Nicole scoffed.

"Oh, like you keep yours?" Joey rebutted.

"What?" Nicole looked incredulously at her friend.

"Don't you and Jay have a little history that hasn't been shared with the rest of the class?" Joey looked at her pointedly.

"Oop," Kiko said with wide eyes as she sipped her wine. Chelle held a smug expression, having an idea of what Joey was referring to.

"I mean, Jay and I have been friends, just not as close as you and Shane," Nicole replied.

"Not even after the wedding?" Joey edged.

"Wow," Nicole blew out, shaking her head.

"Oh?" Kiko raised her brows, befuddled that her bestie had really kept a secret from her.

"OK. OK," Nicole groaned. "At the end of the reception, while we were on the way to the beach, Jay told me how he felt about the situation with Trey, and things got a little heated."

"And?" Kiko sat forward in earnest.

"Heated? That's not what I heard. Apparently it was like the scene out of a soap opera," Joey added.

Nicole laughed, realizing how ridiculous they must have looked kissing and fighting on the beach. She threw up her hands and giggled. "Guilty as charged."

Chelle and Joey laughed, finding it hilarious that Nicole was finally caught in some mess. Especially with her bloodhound nosiness when it came to everyone else. Kiko looked on in disbelief that she seemed to be the only one who didn't know. She thought back to her wedding, remembering how emotional Nicole had been, and wondered how much she had missed.

"Wow," Kiko mused. "And this whole time, you acted like he made your skin crawl. Joey, you might need to take Nick back to Cali with you. Hollywood awaits her!"

They had a few more laughs at Nicole's expense, asking her a million questions. Joey didn't know about Trey's impromptu visit, so they filled her in on that. Then they turned the tables back on Joey, asking about her and Dante. She explained that they were dating exclusively and did a lot of networking together. Kiko gave an exaggerated yawn at that description and Chelle's expression showed that she concurred. They contemplated taking a cab to meet up with the others, but tipsiness had set in, and they quickly forgot that idea when they began talking about the plans for the next night.

"Oh," Chelle called out to no one in particular. "It's almost midnight, and I need to give Nicole her first gift to start her twenty-fifth birthday." She reached for her briefcase that had been resting inconspicuously behind her chair. Pulling out a manilla envelope, she handed it to Nicole.

"What is this?" Nicole was curious as to what kind of gift came packaged that way. She fingered the thick contents, wondering what it could be.
"Just open it," Kiko urged.

Cutting her eyes in suspicion, Nicole twisted the metal bracket closure and opened the flap, sliding out a stapled document. Upon further inspection, she recognized her divorce papers. Gasping, her expression turned serious as she flipped to the back of the document to find not only hers, but Trey's signature finalizing the dissolution of their marriage.

"Oh my God," she sighed, placing a hand over her mouth in shock. She slumped back in her chair, relief overcoming her. She couldn't believe that it was finally over. A strange laugh escaped her throat as she examined the paperwork again to make sure she wasn't dreaming.
"I can't believe it. How?"
Chelle winked. "I told you I would work on it for you. Let's just say it's good to have friends in high and *low* places."

Nicole nodded. Then she felt other emotions vying against her happiness, and the tightness in her throat began to grow. She didn't want to ruin her friend's night with a bout of tears, but the drastic change in her expression was hard to miss.

"You ok, boo?" Joey asked, leaning over to slip

an arm around Nicole, since she was sitting the closest to her.

"I'm fine," Nicole scoffed. "It's silly. I'm so happy." Her tone didn't match her words though, and she hopped up before the water works started.

"Nick," Kiko called to her softly.

"I'm ok," she insisted. "I just need to process this. That's all."

"Don't go," Chelle insisted, but it was too late.

"I'm good. I promise," Nicole said as she moved toward the screen door that led back inside, leaving her friends to wonder if her words were really true.

Chapter 14

Staring at the divorce papers for the thousandth time, Nicole felt herself slipping deeper into her weird mood. She had experienced a sense of relief that it was finally over, and she was free, but that didn't prevent the sadness that followed. Her first love. Her first marriage. Her first everything. There was a time that she almost worshiped Trey, and he had her up on a pedestal. Unfortunately, that wasn't enough to keep them together.

It was a bittersweet victory.

Nicole felt the wetness trickling down her cheek, and realized she was crying. It wasn't an aching feeling, but more like an emptiness. A numbness. The fact that she hadn't even been able to talk to him at the end and had relocated without him knowing was still hard to believe. The defeat in his eyes when Jay had come to her aid. It was all so tragic. Tossing the papers across the bed, she sighed and wiped away her tears.

A soft knock at the door pulled her back to the present. "Come in," she called out as she swiped at her eyes again.

Jay wasn't who she expected to enter, but then again, she shouldn't have been too surprised. He had always been attuned to her moods, and despite her hot and cold feelings about him in the past, he'd always been there for her. Pushing past her guarded nature when even her girls would let her be.

He held out his hand to her, and she grasped it so he could pull her from the bed. His eyes assessed hers and he gave her a warm smile as he wiped a wayward tear away.

"Why are you in here?" He asked, eyes glancing at the scattered divorce papers.
"I just needed to clear my head," she sniffed, trying her hardest to compose herself.
"I have a surprise for you," he said softly.
"Jay," she balked. "That is the last thing on my mind right now."
"Not *that* kind of surprise," he chuckled. When she shot him a disbelieving glare, he threw his hands up. "No funny business. Come on."
"*Jay.*"

"Will you calm yo ass down. You trust me, right?"

She grinned, taking her time to answer. "Yeah. I guess."

"Whatever, Nicky. Just close your eyes. I'll guide you."

Nicole was going to protest again, but she caught herself. She thought about his question and realized that she did trust Jay. He always acted in her best interest even if it was for his benefit. His surprises always cheered her up and were always on time.

The house was quiet as they made their way to the other side of the first floor. She heard the muffled music of slow jams coming from upstairs and figured it was Chelle and Remy. There was also music and lights coming from outside so someone was still out on the porch. Then the scent of vanilla permeated her senses and she inhaled deeper.

"You ready?" Jay asked, removing her blindfold after she nodded.

"Jay," she whispered, covering her mouth in disbelief.

"Go in," he said, placing a gentle hand at her back to guide her.

Their room had been decorated with pillar candles casting the dark room in a soft glow. The bedsheets had been changed from the white bed set to red satin sheets. At least a dozen bouquets of flowers adorned the dressers and night tables, and red rose petals trailed into the ensuite bathroom.

"Keep going," he instructed as he grabbed a remote off the dresser and pressed a button that caused music to come streaming from the room's strategically placed speakers.
"There's more?" The excitement in her voice was reminiscent of a small child.

She took cautious steps toward the bathroom, gasping when she saw that it was also decorated. Even more candles lining the claw foot tub, and more rose petals floated on the surface of a steaming bubble bath. Next to the tub was a tray with a decanter of cognac and a bottle of chilled red wine.

Feeling overwhelmed, she turned to Jay, burying her head in his chest. He held her for a moment, letting her feel whatever she was feeling. He knew that Nicole was sensitive under her tough shell. He'd seen her at her lowest and vulnerable over Trey and figured that whatever she was experiencing couldn't be easy.

"Don't think about anything. I just want you to relax." Jay eased back a bit, sliding a finger under her chin so that he could tilt her heart shaped face upwards. Her slanted eyes were still glassy with unshed tears, but she looked as beautiful as ever in his eyes. "Ok?" He asked, making sure it all wasn't too much for her.

She nodded with a small smile spreading across her face. "Ok."

Jay grinned. "Good."

Turning her to face the tub, he began to undress her. Their eyes locked in the mirror, and she watched on as he slid the shoulder of her dress down until it slipped from her body. He placed chaste kisses to her neck and back, causing an involuntary shiver to ripple through her. His hands glided up her back and unhitched her strapless bra, letting it slip away like her dress. Kissing his way down her back and pushed her panties down until she could step out of them.

Even though she had fussed at the idea of them having sex, Nicole found everything Jay did aroused her. The fact that he was just being affectionate, and not groping her as he normally did, turned her on beyond measure. Of course, the thought of the lengths he'd gone to set this up for her had a huge impact as well.

Walking over to the tub, Jay perched on the thick ledge and dipped a finger beneath the surface to ensure that the temperature of the water wasn't too hot, and then motioned for her to get in. Twisting her hair into a high, tight bun she went to him. When she placed her first leg into the sudsy bath, she groaned at how good the hot water felt. Once she was in and seated, she couldn't help the moan that escaped her lips.

"Oh, this is perfect," she uttered with her eyes closed.
"Feels that good, huh?"

Jay chuckled as he poured them both a drink. Cognac for him, wine for her. Nicole took her wine glass, taking a sip and swirling it around her tongue before she swallowed. It was a sweeter malbec that left a delicious aftertaste on her tongue. Jay took two long swigs of his drink before setting his glass back down.

Slipping an arm beneath the bubbles, he grabbed her calf and massaged downward until he reached her ankle. Then he pulled her leg over the side of the tub so that he could have better access to her foot. When he began to knead her sole, she whimpered in delight. Jay gave her a knowing smile as he went to work until her eyes rolled back and she sunk lower into the water. Whatever pressure point he was working had her pussy pulsing and quivering.

"Aren't you getting in?" Her raspy voice was lazy and languid as she eyed him beneath lowered lids.
"I hadn't planned on it," he replied. "I'm just here to pamper you."
"Get in the tub, Jay." She rephrased her question to a direct statement. It wasn't up for debate. She

wanted his body naked and wet, ASAP.

"Whatever you like," he said mimicking their favorite scene from *Coming to America.*

"Silly," Nicole giggled.

She appraised his body as he undressed, loving the cocky way he returned her gaze, knowing she was enjoying the show. His tattoos always held her attention as she admired the intricately placed symbols of things that were important to him. Of course, basketball was the most prominent. Jay took his time, certain muscles flexing involuntarily as he went. When he pulled down his distressed jeans, his erection tented his Polo boxer briefs. He reached a hand inside to cup his dick, well as much of it as he could before he stripped his underwear away.

Nicole rolled her eyes at his display. "Boy, if you don't get in this damn tub."

"Big boy, that is," Jay corrected her as he let his anaconda swing free. "Rocky Balboa."

"*Rocky Balboa*! Please tell me you've never said that before," Nicole burst out laughing. "As a matter of fact, don't tell me!"

Jay grinned as he joined her in the warm sudsy water, settling behind her and pulling her to rest against his chest. The bubbles were a calming vanilla-lavender aroma which blended nicely with Nicole's almond forward gourmand fragrance. It was her signature scent and he'd come to love it. Especially when it lingered on his clothes or pillows.

"Your ass don't be laughing when I'm struggling to fit him all up in your guts."

"Whatever, Jay," she giggled.

"Yeah, now it's whatever. You're lucky my plan is to relax you. Now lean forward a bit," he replied as he began to knead and rub her shoulders. It felt so good, she forgot about whatever sarcastic retort she was about to deliver, or the fact that Mr. Balboa was firmly pressed against her backside. Jay's hands massaged and tenderized her neck, shoulders, and torso until she felt like she could float away.

"Those hands are lethal," she sighed when he began to massage her temples.

"You're so tense in certain places. I feel like I need to step my game up."

"Step your game up?"

"Yeah. Make sure to take some of that stress away. You been smiling and laughing a lot more lately, and I just want to see more of that. I plan to do whatever I can to make that happen."

Nicole was taken by his words. She was conflicted because her feelings for Jay were deeper than she expected or expressed. Somehow, he had become her rock, and a bright light that let her know how dull her world was before him. The care and concern that he showed her, his attention to her little quirks and the fact that he listened to her all proved to have a fatal effect on her heart.

"You good?" Jay was concerned with her silence. Wondering if he'd pushed too hard.

"I don't know," she sighed. It's weird. You know?"

"I don't think I know, but I can try to understand."

"What I meant is that I know he's out of my life for good now. Two years ago, I couldn't have imagined things would end this way. I'm not as sad about it as I expected, but it feels hollow."

"I guess losing anyone you love would leave a void in your heart," he agreed.

"But we weren't as close as I thought we were. Obviously. It's hard to explain."

"You were with Trey for a long time. Are you regretting your decision?"

Nicole recoiled. "Regret? No."

She put her wine glass on the tray and turned to face him, straddling his hips. Looking into his eyes, she smiled at the purity of his emotions. Behind the women, the tattoos, and the bravado, he was the kindest soul she'd ever met. Jay returned her gaze, and they were both quiet as they assessed each other.

"I need you to know that I don't regret anything," Nicole said.

"Ok."

"You're special to me, Jay. I need you to understand that."

Jay nodded his response, grasping the seriousness of Nicole's confession. For him, feelings had been flowing for her for a long time, but to hear her try to put her own into words meant a lot to him. Especially after the news she received earlier that night. He knew she wasn't the type to profess anything she didn't mean. It probably meant she felt even more than she let on, but he was satisfied with being 'special' for the time being.

He ran his fingers up her back, resting them in the crook of her neck as he guided her to kiss him. They both kept their eyes open, falling deeper into their web of feelings until intensity became too much and Nicole's eyes fluttered shut on a moan. Jodeci's My Heart Belongs to You played in the background, mirroring the depth of passion between them.

Nicole's body rocked against him as her arms wrapped around his neck. Jay's hands slid under her shoulders, holding her as close as possible. The water sloshed around the tub as they got worked up, and her earlier objection to them getting intimate dissolved with each of her whimpers.

Jay was enamored by the way she kissed him. So

slow and painstakingly erotic, he couldn't help getting hard if he tried. And he was trying. His plan had really been to cater to her and help her to deal with receiving the divorce papers, but he wasn't averse to giving her whatever she wanted if she changed her mind.

"Behave," he murmured as he pulled away to catch his breath.

"I am," she whispered. Leaning in, she sucked his bottom lip between her teeth and nibbled.

"Nicole," he groaned. "I'm trying to be good."

"So be good," she purred.

Her hips were swirling perfect circles that caused his erection to slip further and further between the lips of her thick mound. His eyes closed and his head fell back against the tile as she continued to ride him like that. Secretly praying for some sort of slip that would have him sliding into her slick heat. The way her body began to tremble, he knew at least one of them was going to get off. He was more than happy to be used for her pleasure.

Nicole's mouth formed a tight O as her moans increased. Jay focused on her, hungry to see her come because Nicole was so expressive when she became undone. He loved hearing her soft pants and grunts when her climax began to peak, and she knew she was close. She had him bewitched, and he wondered if she knew.

"Shit," Jay groaned. He could feel her pussy flexing and clenching for him.

"Uhh," she uttered as her orgasm eluded her, but she loved the tease.

Jay angled her away from him so that he could have access to her ear, recognizing it as one of her spots. He teased her, kissing and nibbling his way up her neck, stopping to suck the lobe between his lips while his fingers twisted and squeezed one of her breasts. Nicole clutched the side of the tub in response to how her orgasm revved up.

"Oh, yes," she groaned.

She loved the way Jay took his time enticing her. One second, he'd be sucking hard and slow, then he'd switch to licking, the resulting sound causing her to grow wetter and more frenzied. She began to buck with a wild urgency that almost made him lose it.

"That's it, baby. Let it go," he urged.

"Fuck, Jay," she groaned, shocked that she could come that hard without penetration.

"Damn, girl," Jay said. She was shaking in his arms and panting to catch her breath.

"That was intense," she chuckled against his chest.

"I see. I'm a little jealous," he joked.

"Don't worry. I'm gonna take care of you."

"Oh yeah?" Jay raised one brow in intrigue.

"Yeah," she replied. "But not in this bath."

"Nope. I said this was all about you, and since the agenda has changed, I'm not done with you yet.

After they rinsed off and towel dried, Jay led Nicole to the bed.

"Sit," he commanded. She followed his instructions, watching as he went to the closet and returned with a velvet drawstring bag. From it, he pulled out a special candle, a pair of handcuffs and some sort of silicon toy with what she knew to be a cock ring attached to a vibrating bullet. She picked it up to examine it, trying to determine what the other half was for.

"What is this?"

"It's a dual rabbit. This part goes around my dick," he said as he stuck a finger through the cock ring. "And this part will bump up against your clit. We'll both feel the sensations from the bullet."

"Oh," was all Nicole could respond, curious and excited to try it out. Jay was full of surprises, and she loved it.

After lighting the candle, he prepped the toy and placed it next to the bedside table then stood in front of Nicole, who was sprawled out across the bed. His first course of action was to continue soothing her body. Grabbing his cocoa butter lotion on the bedside table, he squirted a large glob into the center of his palm and then proceeded to place dollops all around her body. The massage started with her feet where he took his time with her tender arches and toes. Then he moved upwards, to her calves, her thighs, and her arms.

"Turn on your stomach," he instructed. Then he squirted more lotion directly on her back, purposefully to see her squirm when the coolness hit her skin.

"Hey," she giggled. Her laughs melted into moans when his strong hands began to unravel all the knots in her back and shoulders. Nicole felt herself melting under Jay's touch. He was meticulous, making sure to address each muscle and not moving on to the next until she was satisfied. When he slid his hands down to the base of her back, he paused to admire her natural arch.

"Damn, girl," he couldn't help but murmur. "I don't know which one of us is more blessed. You with all this ass, or me to be able to do this."

Before she could wonder what, he was going to do, Jay was on his knees kissing her ass. Literally. He sprinkled soft smooches across each cheek. Then he spread her open and began to feast away. Nicole had quickly become his favorite flavor.

"Mmm," she sighed.

She didn't think she'd ever tire of how enthusiastic he was about pleasuring her, even though she knew he was enjoying it just as much as she did. His moans while he ate her drowned out her own and turned her on like crazy. By the time he was done his dick was rock hard and poking her back as he crawled up her body. His kisses to her neck and ears made her feel like she was melting away.

"You taste so damn good everywhere," he whispered against her ear, sending shivers all through her and straight to her pussy. He arched her back even more, urging her to push her ass up toward him while he nestled his erection between her luscious cheeks. The way his dick disappeared into their fold when he rocked his hips was a sight that he would see in his dreams. With a light slap, he jiggled each side and enjoyed the ensuing ripples. Then he reared back and easily flipped her on her back, giving her a smug grin when she gasped at the sudden change.

Eager to get the show started, he reached for the toy and the cuffs. The candle had produced enough wax for what he intended. It was the special kind that didn't burn your skin on contact. Nicole wanted to try new things, and he was totally on board with fulfilling her wishes.

He was just about to cuff her first wrist when she stopped him.
"How about you get on your back," she said with a provocative smile.
"But –"

"Don't worry. I won't hurt you," she said before he could protest.

Jay smirked. Even though he had a plan for her, he was curious to see what she had in mind. Doing as she asked, he positioned himself underneath her on his back, lying patiently as she raised each arm above his head and cuffed him. Then she examined the toy, sliding it down his throbbing shaft so that the silicon bunny ears were facing her. Feeling devious, she leaned forward and wrapped her lips around the tip, swirling the head with her tongue.

"Shit," Jay bit out. Not being able to touch her was already proving to be torture.

Then, she reached for the candle, considering which spot she wanted to try first. Knowing where he was most sensitive, she started with the inside of his thighs. She let the melted wax drip and splash over his firm skin, inching closer and closer to his balls. With each pour, he released a long hiss as the liquid first prickled, then quickly cooled against his flesh.

"Nicole," he pleaded. His dick strained against the toy, the veins lining his length rigid and bulging.

Seeing Jay so turned on and helpless made Nicole dizzy with lust. She loved the grunts and groans he made when the hot candle wax grazed his skin, and she couldn't wait to try the joint vibrator. She mounted him, sliding her pussy over the head of his dick and swirling her hips but not going lower. Teasing him. Jay jerked his pelvis upwards, desperate to feel all of her, but Nicole wouldn't allow it.

"Aht. Aht. Aht. I'm in charge now. Be patient."
"Baby," he groaned hoarsely. "Rocky can't get no harder or I'm gonna die."
"You're not gonna die," she smirked while she continued to tease him. This time she descended a little lower but then rose back up until his tip was just inside her. "You like that?"
"Nicky," he growled.
"How about this?"

She clenched her pussy, doing ten kegels on the head of his dick. Jay groaned in agony and slammed his head into the pillows, his body straining with the need to plunge deeper. Nicole carried on with her show, taking his shaft and sliding it across her clit.
"Shit," Jay grunted. "Take these cuffs off.
"What? Aren't you having fun?"
"I'm gonna fuck you so hard," he gritted between his teeth as he stared daggers at her.
"Well, you're not playing fair at all," she pouted as she hit him with another round of kegels.
"Take these shits off me or fuck me. Now! Fuck!"

Nicole bit her lip to keep from laughing, but continued her game until she felt his dick twitching and jumping inside her, and he was begging her to fuck him. Finally, she seated herself fully onto his shaft, squirming as her body accommodated his girth. She barely turned on the toy when she felt the rush of her budding orgasm racing through her. Leaning forward, she released the lock on the cuffs, and they fell away from his wrists. Grunting, Jay grabbed hold of her hips, his fingers digging into her thighs, and pumped upwards to match her pace. Nicole cried out as the sweet bite of pain and pleasure mingled until her body surrendered to him.

"Oh, fuck," Jay barked out. "I'm gonna come."
"Me too, baby," she keened, head thrown back as she grinded her hips.
"*Ah!*" Jay's back strained upwards, and his pelvis jerked violently as he exploded inside her.
"Fuck me," he groaned over and over as she milked him dry. Nicole's body convulsed as if she'd been hit with lightning when her climax finally broke. She moaned his name as she toppled onto his chest.

Chapter 15

"That was crazy," Nicole murmured while she and Jay got dressed after another shower to clean up since there was candle wax and cum everywhere. She was still slightly swooning over their escapade. "And what is that toy called again?"

"A dual rabbit," Jay chuckled.

"Yeah, well we need all the rabbits," she replied.

"Let me find out you a freak for real," he teased.

"You're the freak," she rebutted. "Who's the one that traveled with a velvet bag-o-sex toys!"

"Hey," he said, raising his hands in defense. "You said you wanted to try new things. Don't mock me because I know how to deliver."

"You're so corny," she smirked.

"You got so much mouth now. I bet if I –"

His words were cut off when a thud coming from their patio door startled them both. They glanced at each other, acknowledging that they both heard the noise before Jay crept over to the door to investigate. When he peeped through the vertical blinds, he found Shane and Joey standing with her back plastered against it. He slowly opened it, and she came tumbling in, and he caught her by her arm before she hit the ground.

"Whoa," he said as he steadied her. "What the hell are y'all doing?"
"Shhh," Shane said frantically as he stepped inside and then slid the door shut and closed the blinds.
"What in the world?" Nicole looked at the time and frowned; it was two o'clock in the morning.
Before she could ask another question. Kelly's muffled voice could be heard outside calling out for Shane.
"Jay, I need to holla at you. Come with me outside right quick," Shane said as if everything was perfectly normal.
"Is anyone else still up?" Jay asked as he pulled on a sleeveless t-shirt.
"I think Remy was in the kitchen, but I'm not sure."
"I'll be back," he said to Nicole as he trotted out behind Shane.

Joey and Nicole stood there staring at each other for a moment before they both burst out laughing.
"Girl... What the hell were you doing in the damn

bushes?" Nicole giggled, recalling how ridiculous Joey looked falling into their room.

"I'll tell you all about it once you put whatever that is away," Joey said, pointing to the sex toy that was perched in the middle of the bed.

"Oops," Nicole cackled at her friend's mortified expression. "Hey. It's not like we were expecting company."

There was a knock at the door followed by Chelle peeking her head in before she entered the room. "Jay said y'all were in here up to no good," she said, sipping on a brown drink in a tall glass.

"I didn't think he was serious," she shrieked as she gestured toward the toy that Nicole hadn't had the chance to move yet. That caused Joey to double over in laughter, sliding to the floor in a dramatic fashion.

"Oh, God," Nicole said as she threw the corner of the blanket over to conceal it.

Chelle glanced around the room, taking in the flowers, candles, and music.

"Lookin' real sexy in here. I thought your night was done after the divorce papers."

"I know," Nicole sighed, joining Joey on the ground, and placing her back against the side of the bed. "Jay surprised me with all this."

"Aww," Joey swooned.

"Jay is a sweetheart," Chelle added, sitting next

to Nicole. "We just never got to see this side, I guess."

"This side, or the gun toting side apparently," Joey replied.

"Listen!" Nicole squealed. "When he rolled up to my crib and then pulled his piece out, I almost lost my mind."

"Seems like he been pullin' his piece out on you a lot these days," Chelle remarked.

"Ok!" Joey giggled and gave Chelle a high five. It was clear to Nicole that both her friends were more than a tad bit inebriated.

"Be serious!" Nicole demanded but couldn't help laughing along with them. "I'm gonna need a glass of wine fooling with you two. Where the hell is Kiko?"

She reached up to the bedside table for her wine glass that was still more than half filled.

"She was on the phone with Dom when I checked," Chelle answered.

"I hate that he couldn't make it," Nicole lamented.

"I know. It's gotta be hard with him gone all the time. I don't know how she does it," Chelle replied.

"Yeah. Long distance relationships are rough," Joey sighed.

"You say that like you have experience," Nicole noticed.

"I mean, I work with clients who are away from their families more than they're with them. I see the strain it can cause," Joey explained.

"Good answer," Chelle said with a nod. "But that is the truth. I know Shane is dealing with that now."

"Speaking of Shane," Nicole raised a brow and lowered her voice. "Who is Kelly? When did they become a thing?"

Both Nicole and Chelle looked to Joey.

"Why are y'all looking at me for?"

"Because you're his *best* friend. If anyone knows, it would be you," Nicole said mocking Joey's soft high-pitched voice. Joey rolled her eyes.

"All I know is that they went to high school together. I think she was the girl he took to his senior prom. I guess she has the homely vibe he's going for these days."

"Shade," Chelle chided.

"I think she's pretty," Nicole countered.

"No, I meant she's a homebody. Ready and willing to get barefoot and pregnant for him."

"Wow," Nicole replied.

"I know right," Joey miffed.

"No, wow, you're sounding a little bitter," Chelle clarified.

"Right," Nicole agreed. "C'mon. I've seen– shit we've all seen how you are with each other. And it's obvious there's some feelings here. Why don't you explore where things can go?"

"I told you guys earlier. It's not like that with us. Yes, we are close, but I don't think a relationship would work out.

"You don't think that, or he doesn't?" Chelle asked, remembering a conversation she had with Shane at Kiko's wedding.

Joey's shoulders slumped a bit, but she rebounded with a smile that was a tad too bright.

"We both agree."

"So, since you're gonna make me pull your card, what were yall doing creeping around together earlier?"

"Creeping?" Chelle perked up.

"Yeah. I don't know what they were doing, but they–" Nicole was interrupted when Jay and Remy joined their pow wow bringing drinks and snacks. She huffed, knowing that the opportunity for them to grill Joey about Shane would be put on pause. Even though the entire group could see there was smoke so there was most likely fire where the two were concerned, they would never get the real dirt in front of the guys.

"The last time I walked into a situation like this, y'all were talking about me fake cheating on Chelle. There better not be no drama with my name in it," Remy groaned.

"Just a little girl talk, baby," Chelle said with a sugary smile.

"Yeah. Boring stuff," Nicole added.

"Cool story," Jay said with a grin, making eye contact with Nicole and cutting his eye to convey he didn't buy their story. He handed her a bag of salt and vinegar chips before sliding onto the bed behind her. When it started vibrating under him, he startled, hopping up and pulling the blanket back to reveal the rabbit buzzing away on the bed. "Aw shit."

Joey let a howl of a laugh at the site of Jay dangling the toy as he attempted to switch it off. Remy scrunched up his face and asked, *"What the fuck is that?"*

Chelle succumbed to a fit of giggles, as Joey rolled into her lap with laughter. Nicole slapped her hand across her head in semi-embarrassment when she turned to see what was going on. She handed Jay the velvet bag. "Please, put that away," she urged.

"Nah, for real though," Remy prodded. "Is that what I think it is?"

"It's a dual rabbit," Joey said in-between wheezing and laughing.

"A *what* rabbit?" Remy's brows climbed toward his hairline and Chelle mirrored Joey as she chortled into the palm of her hand.

"Can we just pretend this didn't happen?" Nicole groaned.

I'll put the link in the group chat," Jay chuckled. "Yall laughing now, but you'll thank me later."

The next morning Joey and Kiko cooked for the rest of the house while Nicole was treated to breakfast in bed, compliments of Jay. He slipped out of bed, leaving her fast asleep and returned with a tray of French toast, scrambled eggs with cheese, bacon, and wheat toast. Of course, Kiko made a fresh mimosa for her bestie. When he entered the room, she was just stirring awake.

"Happy birthday, Nicky," he said, waking her completely.

Nicole blinked until her eyes focused on him and she spotted the tray of food and smiled. The smell of bacon made her mouth water.

"Oh my God," she gushed as she rubbed the sleep out of her eyes and sat up so that he could situate the tray on her lap. "Wow, this looks amazing. Thank you."
She puckered her lips for a kiss, and he leaned down and smacked his mouth to hers, then placed a soft peck to her forehead.

"What's this?" Nicole asked as she noticed the rectangle gift box on the side of the tray.
"Jay?" She uttered when he didn't speak, just stood there smiling down her.
"Open it," he urged.

Nicole gave him a sheepish smile as she slipped

off the red ribbon and pulled open the white leather case. Inside was a diamond studded platinum bracelet.

"Jay!" She held it up as she admired the way the
sun rays made it sparkle and shimmer. "This is
beautiful!" She beamed up at him, trying to keep
her tears at bay.

"You like it?" His uncharacteristic shyness made
her heart melt.

"I love you. I love platinum!"

"Yeah, I noticed you don't wear a lot of gold, and
the ankle bracelet that you wear all the time is
platinum," he explained.

"Thank you," she gushed, reaching for him while
trying not to tip over her tray. He leaned over and
kissed her again, pulling away before it started to
get too heated.

"Enjoy breakfast," he said as he straightened up
and headed for the closet.

"Aren't you gonna eat with me?"

Nicole watched as he went to his suitcase and
started pulling out workout clothes. He pulled
off his t-shirt and sweatpants and began to lotion
his body from head to toe. Nicole couldn't even
pretend not to ogle his glorious physique, nor did
she take for granted that he was a top tier specimen of a man. Sometimes she wondered if he
was still seeing other people, but nothing in her
spirit felt that. His time and attention were hers

for the taking.

Jay sat at the edge of the bed to slip on his socks. "I'm going to play ball with the guys. We're meeting up with a couple other Alumni players for a pick-up game."

"Aww," she crooned around a bite of toast. "That sounds like fun. Maybe I'll come watch."

"I thought you wanted to relax?"

"You think these girls are gonna let me?"

"Good point," he chuckled as he pulled on a pair of compression shorts. "Well then you should. You know it's probably gonna get crazy. Especially once people find out that Shane is there."

"Don't act like your ass ain't the main attraction, Jay. I'm sure you'll have more than enough cheerleaders there to see you."

He leaned over and bit the piece of bacon she was about to put in her mouth. "You're the only cheerleader I'm worried about."

"Promise?" She flashed him a sly smile as she recited their inside joke.

"Promise," he said before grabbing his gym bag and leaving.

Just as she thought, Nicole was bum rushed by the girls as soon as Jay and the guys left. First Chelle came in with a pineapple-mango smoothie and a gift box from her and Remy. Nicole gasped when she opened it to find a pair of Tiffany diamond stud earrings like the ones that she'd lost when they were in Turks and Caicos.

"You are determined to make me cry, aren't you?"

"Stop. You know I love you, boo. Even if you did ditch me for Kiko," Chelle teased.

"Now you stop," Nicole chuckled. "I know Joey is your number one. Let's keep it real."

Chelle laughed. "C'mon. Ain't nobody bigger than the group," she quoted the Five Heartbeats movie.

"Shut up," Nicole chortled. "But speaking of Joey. Something is going on between her and Shane.

"Is this de ja vu?" Chelle scrunched up her face in confusion.

"No, in real time," Nicole clarified. "She was outside my patio door last night with Shane and I don't know what they were doing, but she fell into the room when Jay opened the door, and then Shane tried to hide the fact that he was with Joey from Kelly."

"What? She fell in the room?"

"Yeah. Like they were leaning up against the door. Jay saw them, but I haven't had a chance to ask him about it yet. Plus, you know he's gonna cover for his boy."

"True that. But as much as Joey tells me, Shane is the one thing that she won't budge on. She did mention the Kelly situation to me, but I knew about that before she told me because I met her during a zoom meeting, we had regarding a brand deal he was signing. He asked me not to tell Joey and let him be the one to tell her. I don't know what their deal is, but I refuse to let it stress me out."

"I hear you. Something is up with Kiko too, but she keeps brushing me off and focusing on Jay."

"You know Kiko has always kept her and Dom's business out the streets. Nothing new there."

"Yeah, but she usually tells me something. Even if it's an 'I'm just going through it', which is her favorite catch-phrase for relationship drama."

"You know the stress that comes with being with an athlete," Chelle noted. "Or, well you're about to find out."

"Pardon?"

"Oh, so now you're gonna play dumb? Ok, how about this. What are you gonna do if Jay signs with a team in the league?"

"I haven't really thought about it," Nicole admitted. "I think I'm still processing that I'm even seeing Jay, much less thinking about our future. I told him I wasn't ready for anything serious."

"So, you'd be ok with him leaving without you guys having anything established? Because, let me tell you now, that's a bad idea. A dumb idea, even."

"I just got divorced. Isn't it a bit soon to think about the next relationship?"

"Two things can be true Nicole. You can be newly divorced and also considering a new relationship. Stop getting hung up on the optics."

"Wow, you're a legit lawyer now. Can't get nothing by you," Nicole muttered just as Kiko entered with a pitcher of orange juice and a bottle of champagne, followed by Joey who held up two more bottles.

"Guess what time it is," Kiko sang out.

"It's nice out, let's drink out on the patio," Joey proclaimed.

The girls all migrated to the outdoor porch for mimosas and girl talk. Nicole opened the rest of her gifts, a gold bangle bracelet from Kiko and a week's worth of lingerie from Agent Provocateur from Joey, which they insisted she try on. When they were in school, they would always model their clothes and lingerie for each other to make sure everything was sitting just right. Nicole had the bombshell body in the group, and they all cat called and hyped up the sexy ensembles.

Then they decided to crash the guy's pickup game, which turned out to be an event in itself. Just like Jay had said, once the word got out that Shane Duncan was playing with Jay Montgomery and a few other star basketball players, a crowd began to form. Nicole watched Jay, who looked to be in great shape, as he finessed his way up and down the court. Him, Shane, and Remy made a lethal combination, knowing each other so well they could complete no look passes and ally-oops with ease. They put on a show for the onlookers, and the girls even did a few of their choreographed routines from their cheer days.

After the game, they grabbed BBQ from a local food truck that smoked up fresh and tasty meats every weekend. It had been one of their must haves for the trip. Once back at the house, they all showered and lounged around playing Taboo until it was time to get ready for the night. As always, the game got intense because Nicole and Chelle always managed to be on the same team and they were super competitive, but so was Shane and Jay so there was always some sort of clash. It was a wise choice to rent a house because they would have been tossed out of a hotel with their shenanigans.

The Alumni event was being held off campus at a large banquet hall. The group opted to order drivers, since no one had to worry about being the designated driver and arrived in two SUVs. They arrived to a red-carpet reception. Of course, there was a buzz when Shane walked the carpet, and even more murmurs when Jay escorted Nicole. People from their time at FAMU remembered her being married and him as a player. Seeing them together was piping hot tea.

Inside the party was already at full steam. One thing they got from Joey was to be fashionably late versus early and bored. They walked in and after mingling with a few of their classmates, they hit the dance floor. That was one thing about the group. The closest they had to an introvert was Chelle, who could turn up with the best of them if she was in the mood. It had been a while since they had all partied together, and even then, Kiko had left her wedding reception and missed all the real fun.

The real show was Nicole and Jay, who now that there weren't any constraints on their interaction seemed to be a flawless fit. They danced together like they'd been together for years, matching each other's rhythm with ease. He was also strong enough to handle her bodacious body and pick her up like it was nothing. When Say Ahh came on, the group gathered around Nicole and hyped her up for her birthday. Never one to shy away from the attention, she let her body do the talking and showed off her killer moves.

Jay, noticing the eyes of a few of the single guys at the party, felt compelled to let them know the deal. He slid up behind her and catching his vibe, she gave him a devious glance as she bent over and backed that ass up on him. Their friends cheered them on as their steamy chemistry took over, causing a few raised eyebrows and jealous sneers from the crowd. Nicole was the girl that every guy wanted but no one could touch, and Jay was the guy that every girl tried to get to settle down but couldn't. Seeing their bodies gyrating in tune, it was obvious that they were more than friends. Things got a little R-rated when

Splash Waterfalls by Ludacris came on.

Joey and Dante were also attached at the hip, more so him not letting her out of his sight. If he had any ill feelings toward Shane, it didn't show, but he was Joey's shadow for most of the night. Especially after Shane had pulled her out to the middle of the dance floor when Flap Your Wings by Nelly played. That was one of her favorite songs and he didn't understand or care why she was playing the wall. True to her nature, she turned up dancing like she was in a music video, commanding all eyes on her. Chelle was her hype man as she left it all on the floor, dropping low and getting her eagle on. Joey didn't mind the attention, even though she didn't miss the fact that Kelly didn't seem to be having fun as she sat at a table scrolling on her phone while Shane cut up on the dance floor.

And in honor of old times, Nicole insisted they ended the night at the waffle house. Laughing and joking as they reminisced about all the nights they'd ended up there over the years and how they used to call her waffle because she used to order them so much. All in all, Nicole had to admit it was one of the best birthdays she'd had in a long time.

Chapter 16

After her birthday weekend Nicole could sense the shift between her and Jay. First it started with them having dinner together more often. Once she found out that not only could he cook, but he was learning from his grandmother how to make staple Jamaican cuisine, Nicole was more than happy to be his taste tester. Of course, dinner would lead to them spending the night together. The best part was that it wasn't about the sex. Yes, it was off the charts, but sometimes they'd both be too tired, depending on the day they'd had. He was working out more often to get back into his peak professional form and would be physically drained by the end of the day.

The night before he left for Europe was one of those nights. Nicole offered to cook at his place so that he could focus on recuperating and packing. He had done so much for her; she was eager to be able to pamper him. She picked up the ingredients to make his favorite dish of lasagna, which she made very well. Entering his penthouse, which she had her own key to, she was met with the sounds of vintage jazz. Jay was sprawled across his couch with an arm over his head as he slept.

Nicole tried to be as quiet as possible as she moved through the living room to place the groceries in the kitchen and wash her hands. When she returned to the living room, he was still asleep, which was unlike him. Usually, he was at the door to greet her when he knew she was on her way. She watched him for a moment, enjoying his relaxed features, and the sight of the large bulge in his shorts. Something inside her stirred and she felt compelled to place her lips to his, so she leaned over and did just that. Jay inhaled sharply in surprise, his brows furrowed in confusion, then he moaned as he slid his arms around her shoulders and pulled her on top of him.

"Hold on," she giggled as he pressed his face into the crook of her neck and breathed in her scent.

"I was just dreamin' about your ass," he murmured.

"Oh yeah? About what?" She had an idea with the bulge she had noticed when she first walked in.

"Your ass. Literally," he growled as he grabbed

two handfuls. "Shit so fat I can see it in my dreams."

"Shut up," she chuckled as she wiggled out of his grasp. "Don't get any ideas. I'm cooking dinner now. This lasagna will never be made if I let you have your way."

"Boo," he called out after her as she returned to the kitchen. "You're no fun."

"Remember you said that later when I'm lying flat on my back and looking pretty."

"I don't care," he laughed. "I'll just flip you over. Your ass is gonna jiggle regardless."

"I can't stand you," she said, but she was smiling as she unpacked the shopping bags.

"I would mess with you, but I'm starving," he said as he passed her on the way to the fridge, smacking her butt in the process.

"You just can't help yourself, can you?" She turned around to glare at him and he shrugged.

"Guilty as charged," he admitted while peeling a banana and breaking off the tip to put in his mouth.

Nicole shook her head and continued prepping for their meal. There was silence between them for a while until she said, "You must be exhausted. You didn't even hear when I came in."

Jay stretched and sighed. "Yeah. My trainer has intensified my sessions to get me back to NBA level endurance. I'm good while I'm playing, but afterwards is when I feel it, but I guess that comes with age."

Nicole glanced at him, hearing the tiredness in his voice. He didn't seem to be as enthusiastic about the process as he had once been. "Why do you sound so blah about this?"

"I just wonder if this is all a waste of time."

"I'm sure your trainer would have told you if he thought that was the case."

"No, I mean by working to get back in the league."

"I thought that's what you wanted, though?"

"Honestly?" His face was pensive as he tried to formulate a response. "I don't know anymore. I mean, it's not just about my physical readiness. Mentally, I've got to get back into the mindset for traveling, life on the road, the fans. It's a lot to consider."

"Oh," she said, nodding as she absorbed his words.

"And I have these tryouts in Europe, so that's another angle for me to think about."

"How many cities?"

"Istanbul, Milan, and Lyon, France. I'll spend about a week with each team. See how I fit."

"You sound more excited about that," she noted while chopping up fresh basil for her sauce.

"Right? It's weird because for so long it was the NBA or nothin' for me, but now I feel like I need to explore my options."

"I can understand that. Especially when you have options like those. Milan? You know that's up there with Paris for me to visit. Me and Kiko are supposed to plan a trip once we hit our stride."

"Yeah," was his response as he leaned over to kiss her cheek. "I'm gonna be in my office for a few."

"Ok..." She watched him leave, seeming like he had the weight of the world on his shoulders. Reaching for the remote for his sound system, she queued up The Diary of Alicia Keys to listen to while she cooked.

The elephant that had been in the room with them the entire time was their relationship. He didn't mention it, but Nicole knew that she factored into the equation. Heavily. She didn't know how to feel about it, though. Everything seemed to be moving so fast. She didn't like the feeling that niggled at her every time he mentioned going to Europe, but she chose to ignore it.

While they were eating dinner, Nicole's phone dinged, signaling a message from a group chat. Jay was inhaling his food and didn't stop to look at his phone because it never made a sound. Nicole frowned and reached for hers, realizing that his phone was always either on silent or off when they were together. She didn't want to jump to any conclusions, but it bothered her on a visceral level because Trey used to do the same thing.

"Friends," she began to read the message from Chelle out loud. "I've decided to throw a surprise party for Remy's birthday. As you know, or you SHOULD know, his birthday is on January second, so I'd like to throw a New Year's party, that way he won't suspect anything. I'd really love it if all of you could be there. Let me know, and please remember that it's a SECRET. Love ya!"

"New Years? Damn. That's in the middle of my trip," Jay said, finally giving his fork a break.

"I figured you'd be back by then," Nicole replied. "You said three weeks?"

"Nah, I'll be with each team for a week, but I'm gonna need rest and travel time in between. I'll be gone for about a month and a half."

"Oh, wow," Nicole said, not sure why she was feeling so dejected. She'd known that he planned to travel to Europe, but something about hearing him say he would be gone for over a month made her feel some type of way. "So, you'll be gone for Thanksgiving, Christmas, and New Years?"

"Now why do *you* sound like that?" Jay picked up on the change in her mood immediately.

"Huh? No, I'm good. Just didn't realize you'd be gone that long. That's all."

"Aww," Jay said, putting down his fork and reaching over to caress her face. "You're gonna miss me."

"What?" She scoffed as if it were a ridiculous sentiment.

"Oh. So, you're not gonna miss me?" Jay's eyes twinkled with amusement as he taunted her.

Nicole glared at him before rolling her eyes and taking a bite out of her garlic bread. "I mean, maybe a little," she replied.

He stood up, towering over her as he took her fork and toast and placed them on the table before pulling her out of her seat.

"What are you doing," she balked as he corralled her into his arms.

"It's ok, Nicky. Im'ma miss you too," he said.

"Oh, brother," she groaned at his theatrics. "I hate that you call me Nicky!"

"Which means you secretly love it," he laughed. "I think I'm really cracking your code."

"Is that so? Well, what else do you know?"

"Well," he started and kissed her forehead. "I know you love when I do that. The smug little smile you get warms my heart."

"Whatever," she said, but she was smiling.

"And," he continued. "You love it when I do this." He pulled her closer and nuzzled his face in her neck. She couldn't even help the resulting sigh if she tried.

"Um hmm. What else?"

"Well, we both love this," he whispered as he softly brushed his lips back and forth against hers as he angled his head for a kiss.

"Mmm mmm," she protested as she tried to turn her head away. "My breath smells like garlic!"

"Gimme those lips," he demanded, holding her

head in place. "I'm not a vampire. I don't care 'bout no *damn* garlic."

"Feeling Me Feeling You" played in the background as she relented, puckering her lips tightly as she offered up a chaste kiss. Jay pressed his mouth to hers, once, twice, and then a third time before he began to nibble on her bottom lip.

"Open," he whispered.

Nicole sighed and did as he said. She couldn't resist his affection, finding that it had a narcotic-like effect on her soul. He had totally cracked her code because everything he did was her favorite. She just wouldn't admit it out loud.

Jay tilted her head back, deepening the kiss as she slid her arms around his neck. He moaned deeply when she snaked her tongue into his mouth, garlic be damned. What started out as a gentle embrace was morphing into something hot and passionate. Nicole could feel his thick arousal against her belly and her core tightened. Dinner was going to have to wait.

Nicole gasped when, with a groan of urgency, Jay dipped down and grasped her just under her ass, picking her up and wrapping her legs on either side of him. He took a few steps until her back was up against the wall, and her breath hitched at the coolness against her bare shoulders.

Her hands caressed and massaged the back of

his head and neck, resulting in soft moans as he pressed his erection into her mound. It strained against his clothes, and he grunted in agony, shoving his basketball shorts down until it sprang free. Then he gathered her dress, pulling it up around her waist. He slipped a finger into her panties, finding her already drenched, and then ripped them away.

"Damn, baby. You ready for this dick?"
"Mmm, yes," she moaned. Her hands slipped down to his back, and her nails scored his skin through his thin t-shirt as she bristled with the need to feel him. "Fuck me. *Please*," she begged. No foreplay needed.

As if reading her mind, Jay was already positioning the head of his shaft at her entrance, swirling it in her juices before sinking as deep as he could inside her. They both cried out at the contact, her from the satisfaction of feeling filled, and him at how her walls rippled and gripped his dick tightly.

"You feel so fuckin' good," he whispered hoarsely against her ears. "Your pussy creaming all over my dick."
"Ahhh," she keened as a sharp orgasm formed deep in her core. The ache driving her to squeeze and clench around his girth as he fucked her slow. The agony of how good it felt mixed with

her need for him to fuck her harder made her feel like she would lose her mind.

"Jay," she gasped when he titled his pelvis upward and hit her spot. The way he arched his back in a methodical stroke that caressed her g-spot on the front end, and her clit when he filled her to the hilt. Her body trembled, increasing with every thrust.

"Wait," she whimpered, not used to the intensity that she was feeling.

"You can take it," he encouraged before slamming into her again.

"Jay," she cried out, holding onto him with a death grip despite pleading with him to wait.

"Relax," he gritted through his teeth. "I got you. Don't fight it."

Slowly he lowered her to the ground, placing her on her back and hovering over her. He spread her legs wide apart as he continued to ease in and out at a steady pace. He palmed her clit at just the right pressure until it felt like a dam was bursting inside of her. Her fingers dug into the skin of his arms as she grunted and warm fluid gushed out of her.

"Oh God," she cried in horror, feeling like she'd lost all control of herself, and was drifting away on some sort of cloud. Her vision blurred as she heard Jay saying words she couldn't quite make out.

"That's right baby. Squirt all over this dick," he grunted. His back bucked as he fought to hold on to his own release, not ready to end the magical moment, and loving the feel of her cum and how it coated his dick and spilled out between them. He'd known since the first time he was with her that he would make her squirt, and the fact that it happened was almost as good as losing his virginity all over again.

"What the fuck," she mumbled, regaining a bit of her senses. Her hands, now grasping limply to his wrists, moved toward where their bodies were joined, and she slowly examined the scene. She was surprised at the amount of sticky fluid coming from her.

Jay grabbed both hands and placed them on his chest above his nipples. They weren't his most sensitive spot, but when he was as aroused as he was, teasing them added to the tension building inside of him. He leaned down and kissed one of her hands, lapping her essence off her fingers.

"You're so nasty," she whispered, still overcome from her climax, yet feeling another one brewing.

"Oh, shit. *Jay!*"

"Um hmm. I feel it. I'm coming too," he moaned.

He held back as long as he could, but when

she tightened around him again, he tipped forward as his own release detonated like fireworks through his loins. His lips dragged across the skin of her cheeks until he found her mouth and kissed her with a fierceness that took her breath away.

They both lay there, panting and spent. Jay's head had settled into his favorite spot at the base of her neck, and Nicole absently traced random patterns along the skin of his back. She began to wonder about her marriage, and whether she'd ever really been in love with Trey, or merely infatuated with him. Besides the fact that the sex was stunningly mind blowing, she'd never felt the depth and range of emotion that she experienced with Jay. It was like comparing a first-generation cell phone with a tenth-generation iteration. Everything just seemed more vivid and bold. More satisfying.

Unfortunately, right behind all those good feelings was her uncertainty for their future. He had a huge decision to make between the NBA and the Euro league, but either choice meant things between them would have to change. Even if he didn't go to Europe, he could be picked up by a team in another state which would result in a long-distance situation, which she wasn't ever going to entertain again. And if he went to Europe, they were as good as over.

Just like Jay was weighing his options, she thought about hers. Her business was just starting to take off and a long-distance situation wouldn't be viable even if she considered it. They weren't even official, so moving with him was also unlikely. Thinking back to her suspicions on why he always kept his phone on silent, she wondered if this was all temporary for him. Maybe he always knew he'd be leaving, and never had any intentions of them being anything real. The thought enraged her.

"What's wrong?" Jay asked, feeling her body stiffen underneath him.
"Nothing," she lied. "This floor isn't very comfortable."
"Oh," he chuckled. "Sorry. I think my legs might be working now."

He struggled to get up, eventually just rolling over onto his back so that she could get up. She made a beeline for the bathroom, feeling tears forming as her throat tightened. It was as if the pieces of a puzzle were coming together, and she was seeing the big picture. Jay had agreed to her dating other people as long as she only fucked him. Now that he got what he wanted he could go off and gallivant all over the world if he wanted to, and the fact that the thought made her sick to her stomach was alarming.

Once inside the bathroom, she closed the door

and paced back and forth, careful to avoid her reflection. She wasn't prepared to see the dumb bitch that would be reflected back at her. The tears that she'd been fighting to keep at bay began to trickle down her cheeks and she shuddered as she tried to calm down. Part of her felt like she was probably over-reacting, but part of her wasn't so sure.

Whipping the door back open to get her stuff and leave, she froze when she found Jay waiting outside the door with his arms folded.

"What's going on with you?"
"I'm just tired."
"You don't want to finish dinner? I put the plates in the microwave."
"Nah. I lost my appetite. I think I'm just gonna head home.
"*Home?*" His tone was incredulous. "Why aren't you spending the night?"
"I figure you probably need your space, and don't you have to pack?"
"Nicole," he deadpanned. "What are you doing?"
"I'm doing what I should have been doing."
"Which is?" His tone was calm and even while hers was becoming increasingly agitated, and that pissed her off.
"Which is," her voice raised slightly, and she took a deep breath to lower it. "Which is to sleep in my own bed."
"Because?"

"Because! All this spending the night and eating together has blurred all the lines and now you're leaving. So that's it."

"I'm coming back, Nicole. Why are you acting like I'm moving away tomorrow?"

"Don't do that," she spat.

"Don't do what?" He raised his hands in confusion.

"Don't talk to me like I'm crazy."

"Nicole, you're acting a little crazy. Can you just tell me what's bothering you instead of tossing all this nonsense at me."

"Oh. It's nonsense? Ok." She brushed past him toward the kitchen to grab her purse. Then she slipped her feet into her Fendi slides. Jay was leaning up against the front door waiting on her next move.

"Why are you doing this?" The confusion in his voice caused something inside her to crack, but she was too worked up to slow down.

"I just need to think. In my own space."

"Why do I feel like you're breaking up with me? And I don't even know what I did."

"We can't break up, because we were never together," she snipped.

"Is that what you wanted?"

"No. I wanted to date and have my freedom. Remember? And you wanted to fuck."

"And is that what we've been doing? Because I thought we were both enjoying what was happening between us, and now you're coming at me like I did you foul."

"Who knows what you're up to. Maybe that's why you keep your phone on silent all the time. Keep me from finding out about your other hoes."

"My other hoes?" He laughed, not because it was funny, but because it was ridiculous. "So, now you're just one of my hoes? Are you being serious right now?"

The fact that he could find any humor in the situation didn't help to calm her down but produced the opposite effect. She felt the tears resurfacing again.

"Could you just let me leave?"

"Are you jealous?" He sounded like the idea just hit him. "Nicole, I'm not seeing anyone else. If that's what you're thinking."

"Then what do you have to hide? Why do you keep your phone faced down? Why don't we go out? We're always either at your place or my place. Why were you so ok with letting me date other people?"

"Because I'm following your lead!"

The sudden outburst caught her off guard and she jumped back.

"I'm doing things at your pace because you act like you don't give a fuck about anything and I gotta decipher your feelings because you won't just tell me how you feel. Damn!"

"Well, I guess my feelings don't matter. You're either going to the NBA or playing abroad, and I can't do long distance again."

"You know, there's another option that you left out. I might not do either and focus on my other business ventures. I don't have to go away at all."

"Then what? I don't want you to throw away your opportunities for me. I would always wonder if you regretted it. Ball is life. It's friggin' tatted on your chest. And when we spoke earlier, you only mentioned the two options, so that's what you really want."

"Nicole, please." He reached out and gathered her hands in his. "Please stop. Stop talking as if you've been lied to or played. I've been honest and open with you about my every move. Whatever is going on in your head isn't true."

"I mean, it's not like you didn't know you might be leaving this entire time. Right?"

"So, that's what you think? That I was just trying to fuck? And fine. If that is true, isn't it what we agreed to? Why are you upset?"

"It's my bad. I caught feelings. Silly me."

"And what's wrong with that?"

"Because it's a waste of time. Please. I just want to go home."

"So, what happens when I come back from Europe?"

"We go back to being friends I guess."

He shook his head and dropped her hands. "Back

to being friends. Are you for real?"

When she just shrugged, he realized that Nicole was committed to her stance.

"Ok," he said. Moving out of her way.

"Ok?" She was shocked that he let it go but recovered quickly. "Thank you."

She brushed past him and opened the door. Like a fool, she glanced back at him and the fire she saw in his eyes gave her pause, but it didn't change the fact that they would come to an end eventually, and she had learned it was better to rip the Band-Aid off. She didn't expect the emptiness she felt when his door closed behind her.

Chapter 17

When Nichole went into the office the next day, Kiko was all over her.

"Good morning, butter cup," Kiko greeted her when she stepped into their suite.

"Hey," Nicole managed to grumble as she slipped off and hung up her denim jacket.

"Ew. You know, most people are usual more cheerful after getting their back blown out all night."

"Ok," was all the energy she could muster up.

Kiko frowned. "What's wrong with you?"

"I just have a lot on my mind," Nicole sighed as she powered up her laptop. "Did we get the updates from Gerrard? I want to work on our media and press kits for our brand roll-out."

"Nicole?" Kiko finally took a good look at her friend and noticed the bags under her eyes. "Ok. Either you're sick or you've been crying."

"I'm fine, Kiko. Can we just focus on work, please?"

"*Um*, no the hell we can't. Not when you look and sound like that. What happened?"

Knowing that Kiko wasn't going to let it go, Nicole sighed again. "I should have called out sick."

"Then I woulda shown up at your house and we'd be right where we are now. So just start talking."

Nicole felt silly trying to explain what she'd done. When she woke up the next morning, she still agreed with her decision, but not necessarily how she went about it. "I ended things with Jay last night."

"What? Why?" Kiko's tone matched Jay's level of confusion and her stomach churned.

"I let things go too far. He's got all these major decisions coming up and I'm not down to do long distance, so we were headed nowhere fast."

"So? You just ended it? What did you say? What did *he* say?"

Nicole dropped her head in her hands, then slid her fingers upwards to massage her temples. She took a deep breath before launching into the events of the night before. Starting with their talk while she prepared dinner and ending with her walking out the door. To her credit, Kiko listened without interruption or commentary, but once Nicole was done talking, she went on a tirade.

"Girl? What? You basically made up a whole scenario and used it as an excuse to break up! *Why?*"

"We weren't together," Nicole clarified.

"Oh, give me a break, Nicole. Come *on.* Call him and apologize. Tell him you were trippin."

"No!" Nicole grabbed Kiko's hands as she attempted to reach for her cell phone. "Just leave it. I know how I did it was a little crazy, but –"

"A little crazy? VERY crazy!" Kiko interjected.

"But like I said. I'd rather end it now then wait for him to tell me he's leaving."

"Wow," Kiko said, shaking her head. "I'm sorry, but I think you're being ridiculous. Jay isn't even like that. I don't know why you keep selling yourself short." She flopped down into her chair, baffled by her friend's behavior.

"Selling myself short?"

"Yeah. Like you don't know that you're special. Maybe you do need some time before you start dating, because this situation with Trey has really done a number on you."

Nicole bristled at Kiko's words. "So, I'm supposed to ignore the similarities? Especially that shit with the phone."

"So, you'd rather it be ringing off the hook while you're sitting there trying to chill, or in the middle of fuckin'? You want to see the messages of the random groupies, or chicks he used to mess with sending him pussy pics, or asking to suck his dick?"

"*Huh?*"

"Dom is married, and these chicks will stop at nothing to try and get to him. I've seen the DMs on his social media and it's really sickening. I don't even want to imagine what it's like for Jay. Especially with the fact that there are women who have been with him clamoring for that number one spot. Meanwhile, you're throwing it away."

Nicole leaned back in her seat as she digested Kiko's words. She'd never considered things from that perspective and had no response. Kiko had a point. The thought that Jay might have been protecting her, not hiding things from her made what she did seem even sillier.

"Yeah. You didn't even think about that," Kiko sighed.

"So, now what?" Nicole wasn't sure what she should do because the fact remained that they would eventually face a possibly insurmountable hurdle regarding his career choice.

"Now he gets on a plane as a single man headed for Europe, free to do whatever he pleases," Kiko shrugged.

"Well, thanks for helping me feel better," Nicole huffed.

"Don't blame me for this mess. I'm trying to help you fix this shit, but I know your stubborn ass won't."

Kiko's phone rang and she dropped the conversation to talk to Joey who was helping them with a marketing campaign, leaving Nicole with her own thoughts. Looking at the clock above their whiteboard, she wondered if she had time to catch him before his flight. On an impulse, she grabbed her phone, motioning to Kiko that she was going to grab some coffee from the shop a few doors down. When she stepped outside, she looked at her phone and pulled up Jay's contact info. She considered whether she should call him or send him a message wishing him a safe trip, and before she knew it her finger was sliding across the call icon. Her heart dropped when the call went straight to voicemail. She took that as a sign to let it go and went to get her hazelnut latte.

By the time Thanksgiving rolled around, Nicole's mood hadn't improved. She hoped that going home and spending time with her parents would help, but as she laid in her childhood bed, she felt more adrift than ever. Her emotions had been jacked up since she broke things off with Jay, and not a day passed that she didn't question whether she had made a mistake. The consensus from her friends was that she had.

Her mother and father were split on their opinions on the situation, and both spoke their mind over Thanksgiving dinner which made Nicole glad she was an only child. Her mother understood her reservations about his future and needing to take some time to herself after Trey, but her father disagreed. He was a fan of Jay, especially after hearing how he had protected Nicole when Trey popped up. His stance was that Jay's actions had shown her exactly how he felt about her and that sometimes women let the voices in their head cloud them from what's happening in reality. Then her parents had launched into their age-old argument about men and women in relationships, from which she had excused herself and gone to her room.

"Knock! Knock!" Chelle's muffled voice came from the other side of the door.

"Enter," Nicole called back, sitting up and smoothing her ponytail.

Chelle burst into the room with a tray from Dunkin Donuts and a backpack, and Joey followed behind her with a large box of donuts. Nicole ached at the sight of her friends and unexpectedly burst into tears. She realized how sad she really was.

"Aww," Joey crooned, as Chelle was already pulling Nicole into a hug.

"It's gonna be ok, babe," Chelle said as she rubbed Nicole's back. Joey came up on the side of them, resting her head on Nicole's shoulder.

"Don't cry, Nicole," was all she could manage. Nicole was usually the tough one, but ever since her marriage broke down, she'd been extra sensitive. This was only the second time Joey had ever seen her cry and it was still shocking. "We brought donuts and hot chocolate."

"And movies," Chelle added.

"Oh my God, I'm so silly," Nicole sniffed as she swiped at the tears trickling down her face.

"You're not silly. Just a little emotional," Joey replied.

"And a little self-sabotaging," Chelle noted.

"Really, Chelle?" Joey chuckled.

"But we're here to help," Chelle quickly added.

"It's ok. I am sort of a mess, I guess," Nicole replied, taking the jelly donut that Joey handed her.

"It happens to the best of us," Chelle chuckled. She flopped onto Nicole's microsuede loveseat with her glazed donut and hot chocolate. "Wanna talk about it?"

Nicole swallowed a bite before replying. "Not really."

"Well, I was only being nice by askin'," Chelle replied. "I've heard Jay's side. I'm kinda miffed that you didn't call me, but I know how you are."

"You spoke to Jay?" Nicole asked at the same time Joey asked, "What did Jay have to say?"

"So, we *are* going to talk about it," Chelle confirmed.

"Like I have a choice," Nicole scoffed.

"We promise not to hurt your feelings like Kiko," Joey added.

"She didn't really hurt my feelings. Just put her entire foot in my ass. That's all."

"Well Jay was upset. He said he felt totally blindsided because you never mentioned any issues. And I guess he was confused because of the timing?" Chelle raised her brows at Nicole in question of what that could mean.

"What about the timing?" Joey asked as she munched on a cream filled donut.

"I can't." Nicole hid her face, embarrassed.

Joey and Chelle exchanged a quizzical glance.

"What happened?" Chelle prodded.

"I squirted for the first time," Nicole blurted out.

"Wow, ok!" Chelle replied as Joey said, "Oh shit!"

"But what does that have to do with you cutting him off?" Joey asked, confused.

"I don't know. It's like one minute I was delirious and the next I started thinking and all these thoughts started floating around my head about him possibly seeing other people, and the fact that he hides his phone screen, and that maybe it was always a temporary thing for him. Next thing I felt like I was in a rage," Nicole said as she picked at her cuticles. The thought of the night's events twisting her into a knot. She couldn't stop envisioning the look on his face when she gushed all over him. It haunted her most nights until she had to touch herself just to ease the longing for him.

Chelle and Joey were both quiet after she finished. Chelle smirking while Joey looked off to the side, trying not to laugh.

"What?" Nicole asked when she noticed they hadn't responded.

"So, that man turned you out and you lost your damn mind," Chelle chortled. "He had you feelin' so good it pissed you off!"

Joey had tears streaming down her face as she tried to hold back her laughter, but Chelle's commentary had her weak.

As mad as she wanted to be, Nicole couldn't help but be amused at her friend's reactions. She wasn't used to being the butt of the joke but had to admit that Chelle was right.

"I did feel like my soul left my body," she admitted with a guilty smirk.

"You had a system failure," Chelle giggled.

"Malfunction," Joey said in a robotic tone. "Does not compute. Does not compute!"

Chelle fell out laughing, reaching for Nicole's leg as she tugged on her sweatpants. "Malfunction," she repeated and then laughed heartily as Joey continued to giggle.

"I don't really appreciate this," Nicole said, but she was trying not to laugh herself. "Will y'all be serious!"

"Ok. Ok," Chelle huffed, trying to calm down. "Joey, be serious. Please."

"Me?" Joey laughed. "I'm not the one out here acting like a gremlin when someone feeds it after midnight!"

"Joey! *No!*" Chelle fell back, laughing as she imagined Nicole on a rampage and Jay trying to understand why she was so upset. "Oh my God. Poor Jay!"

"I thought you were supposed to be here to help. I'm about to kick both of you out," Nicole cried.

"Alright," Chelle repeated a few times, really trying to get a hold of herself.

"I'm sorry, Nick. That shit is hella funny. I could only imagine Jay's face while you were going off. He probably hadn't even recovered all his brain function yet and had to deal with you spazzing out."

"It was pretty tragic," Nicole mused.

"Ok, but what matters is what you're going to do about it," Chelle said, finally regaining a modicum of her composure.

"I don't know. I tried to call him before he left, but I must have been too late. Besides he didn't even try to stop me or call me. Maybe I'm right."

"You are absolutely not right," Chelle said.

"Not even close," Joey chimed in. "Jay is a lot of things, but he wasn't playing you."

"I'm going to say something that you may or may not agree with but needs to be said. Jay is not Trey. It's like you're forgetting that he's been your friend, a good friend all this time and your fear is distorting your perception of him to match what you've been dealing with. Maybe this time apart will be a good thing because I think your emotions are all tangled up.

Nicole nodded solemnly. "You're probably right."

"Jay is one of the good ones," Joey said.

"And as your friend and his friend I'm gonna tell you that you fucked up."

"Damn," Joey hissed.

"Well," Chelle shrugged, flashing an incredulous glance.

"I know," Nicole shocked them both by admitting.

"Damn, now I almost feel bad for being straight up. It's gonna be ok, boo," Chelle said, wrapping her arms around Nicole again.

"Well, the good thing is that it's not like you won't have an opportunity to talk things out. You can't avoid one of your best friends," Joey reasoned.

"Yeah, but I feel stupid calling him while he's in Europe. I'll wait to see if he wants to talk to me," Nicole said.

"Or we can stalk his social media!" Joey pulled out her i-Pad and opened her Facebook app. She scooted closer so that they could all see the screen. She didn't have to scroll long before a picture of Jay in a French cafe popped up.

"Aww, he looks so sad," Joey pouted.

"He does not look sad," Nicole disagreed.

"Eh." Chelle scrutinized his expression again.

"That is that *'I'm fake deep'* face he does. Cut it out," Nicole balked.

"I think you're right," Chelle chuckled. "Damn, look at all the comments!"

"These chicks outchea parched," Joey replied.

"This isn't helping," Nicole said, as she looked away. She already missed him, and the hundreds of comments from his female admirers were making her jealous all over again.

"Hold up," Joey said as she turned away with the device. When "You Got It Bad" by Usher started to play, Chelle began to chuckle again.

"Don't start," Nicole warned. "What are you guys doing here anyways? How did you get away from Remy? And how come I didn't know Joey was coming to New York?"

"Ah, there she is," Chelle joked. "Remy has a house full of cousins, and my parents went on a cruise."

"My mother has too many kids to come visit me in L.A. and I wasn't in the mood to be depressed by a trip to Oakland. Dante went to see his family in North Carolina, so I decided to come see my peeps and jumped on a flight last night."

"A last-minute flight from Cali to NY? Those coins must be stacking," Nicole ended with a whistle.

"Business is good," Joey quipped.

"Well, I'm glad you came. You guys made my day," Nicole said in a rear moment of vulnerability.

"Aww me too," Joey said as her and Chelle converged on top of Nicole. "I would have missed squirt-gate if I hadn't!"

"Squirt gate?" Chelle cackled.

"Get out my house," Nicole cried even though she was laughing.

That night after her friends left, she sat in the family room flipping through her mother's photo albums. She was particularly drawn to the pictures of her parents, and their progression over the years. Her father was an outwardly stern man, but he had a gentleness that shone through, especially where his wife and baby girl were concerned. Whenever they posed, he always had a hand to her mother's back, and if she was in the picture a hand on Nicole's shoulder. That love and protection provided a sense of security, and it dawned on her that Jay made her feel that way.

In the newer albums were pictures of Nicole during high school and college. Pictures of her dance recitals, graduations, and the few times her parents came to visit her in Tallahassee. They were adamant about meeting all her friends, and wanted to make sure she was staying focused. Her father had always been fond of Remy and Jay, despite her grumblings about him being a player. His opinion was that they had the makings of a good family man, and they would grow out of their boyish ways. He wasn't wrong.

"What are you doing in here?" her father said, startling her.
"Dad! You scared me," Nicole complained.
"Excuse me for trying to eat a slice of pie in my own living room. What was I thinking?"
"Silly," Nicole chuckled. She watched him as his tall frame got comfortable on the couch beside her and handed her the plate for her to take a taste of his pie.
"It was good seeing the little ladies today. I'm glad you guys are staying close."
"You're gonna have to stop calling us little la- dies, dad," she chuckled. "But yeah. Those are my girls."
"And how's Kiko holding up?
"She's alright, I guess. We're going through it at the moment," Nicole admitted.
"You know that's your sister. What you guy's bickering about this time?"

Over the years, Nicole and Kiko butt heads be- cause they both had a tendency to be blunt, un- like Chelle and Joey who know how to be more diplomatic about their opinions.
"Not really bickering. She's annoyed at how I handled things with Jay, and I didn't like the way

she handled me. Nothing that won't blow over."

"Well, you make sure. Life is different when husbands and other stressors become a factor. Maybe she's going through her own shit. I can't imagine being married to a professional athlete is easy."

"She kind of said something to that effect. When I complained about Jay's phone she went on a rant about the number of other women trying to get his attention. Out of all of us, she's the most secretive about her personal stuff, it just isn't as obvious because she's outgoing and bubbly. I told her I was gonna work remote and stay up here until after New Year's. She didn't seem too happy about it."

"You guys will kiss and make up. Just remember to cut each other some slack. You're not teen-agers sharing a dorm room anymore."

"Aww. Thanks dad. Those gray hairs aren't for nothing, huh?" She teased him by plucking at the silver hairs in his mustache.

"I bet I can still whoop your butt in Dominos," he taunted.

"Bet!"

Chapter 18

Being back in New York was just what Nicole needed. She was able to catch up with her cousins and friends and spend more time with Chelle. Spending time with her parents had really helped her to not only deal with her current personal mess, but also her divorce from Trey. Her mom was especially helpful in encouraging Nicole to create her own closure since it wasn't possible to communicate with Trey. Neither of her parents thought it was wise for her to even try to reach out to him for any reason.

Helping to plan Remy's birthday party kept her busy, and from totally obsessing over Jay. She still hadn't called him, and he hadn't reached out to her. His social media posts of various pics of him in charming social settings, or while he practiced with the team was her only lifeline to him. He was in France, and it looked like he was really enjoying himself.

A pang of sadness ricocheted through her chest at the thought of him deciding to move to Europe and her not seeing him for long periods of time. She couldn't believe she let herself fall into this situation, catching feelings when she should have been having fun and keeping things casual. She blamed Vance for being such a bad date that she was leery about trying it again, and agreeing to Jay's proposition in the first place.

Kiko was another sore spot for her because even though they had to speak regarding work, she kept it short and sweet with Nicole. An outsider wouldn't notice that anything was wrong, but it was obvious to Nicole that her friend was acting strange. When Nicole tried to bring up their conversation about Jay, Kiko brushed it off and changed the subject. Nicole wasn't going to push her; she would just deal with her face to face.

Joey had really surprised her by checking in with her more often, despite being busy with her growing clientele. Even if she didn't call, she sent a cheerful text or joke each morning to set the tone for the day. She seemed to really understand Nicole's mood. Nicole found herself looking forward to it.

Christmas was relatively uneventful. Now that she was grown her parents didn't see the need to put too much effort into the holiday, both admitting that they were super festive for her benefit but were relieved when she moved away from home, and they didn't have to worry about it anymore. They still decorated and had a tree with presents underneath, but the big family dinner and Christmas Eve party seemed to be a thing of the past. Nicole was fine with that because she wasn't in the mood to entertain a bunch of people anyway. Chelle and Remy went on a trip for her mother's birthday, so she wasn't even in town for Nicole to visit.

New Year's Eve arrived in a blink.

"I can't believe I've been up here for a month," Nicole marveled to Chelle as they got dressed in the hotel where the party was being held. Remy thought he was meeting Chelle and Nicole in the city for a New Year's Eve party. They had to pull his arm to convince him to travel to the city because he hated all the holiday traffic. Of course, Chelle's begging had him folding in no time. Nicole also pleaded her case that she wanted to spend time with her bestie since she was in town.

"I know. Time is really flying," Chelle remarked as she scrutinized the fit of her dress in the mirror. "Are you at least feeling any better?"

Nicole sighed. "I guess so. I miss him. A lot."

Chelle glanced over at Nicole and gave her a small smile. "Aww. I'm sure you guys will talk when he gets back to Florida. Remy spoke to him, and he says he's already missing the food."

"The food, huh," Nicole said, sounding defeated.

"You know what?" Chelle chuckled. "I'm not entertaining your moping today. Let's get some pep in our step for this party. You good?"

Nicole laughed. "Ok. I'll do better."

"Thank you." Chelle smacked Nicole's ass as she reached around her to grab her makeup bag.

"I actually can't wait," Nicole replied. "I know we're gonna have so much fun."

"Yes, we are! Kiko and Joey are on their way to the hotel now. They'll meet us downstairs once they get changed," Chelle explained.

"Cool." Nicole nodded.

When they were ready, Chelle asked Nicole to go meet with the manager on the status of the banquet room they were renting while she checked in with the DJ, who needed instructions about where he could park and bring in his equipment. She wanted to make sure everything was set up and ready to go and they could access the room so she could add a few finishing touches. Happy for something to do, Nicole went down to the lobby.

They weren't too far from Times Square, so the lobby was vibrating with the energy of the pending ball drop and festivities leading up to it. She stepped gingerly in her five-inch heels, stopping outside the doorway that led to their banquet room to text Chelle to bring down her flats. She knew her feet wouldn't hold up all night. The door opened, and what she saw took her breath away.

"Did you miss me?"

Jay stood there decked out in a tuxedo that rivaled anything Bruce Wayne ever wore. He grinned as Nicole's mouth widened in shock at the sight of him, and his warm smile melted her heart. This time the tears that sprang up in her eyes were happy. She realized she was happy to see him and nothing else mattered.

"Jay," she whispered. "What are you doing here?" "Is that a yes? I'm gonna need confirmation because I'm not taking anything else with you for granted." He extended his hand to her.
"Yes," she nodded as she placed her hand in his.
"Good. Cause I missed you like crazy," he said softly. "Stubborn ass."
"So, I've been told," she said against his mouth as he leaned down and pressed his lips to hers. She sighed in relief at the feel of his strong arms encircling her. Her tears flowed as the ache of

longing for him subsided along with the fear of never feeling them again. Her arms clung around his neck as she strained closer to him. He leaned backwards, lifting her off her feet as he hugged her tight. When he set her back down, his grin made her laugh.

"I heard there was a party here tonight, or something," he joked.
"Oh, shit. That's right. I'm supposed to be meeting up with the manager," she blurted out as she reached for his hand and led him down the hall. "Chelle will kill me if I don't make sure everything is just right."

When she pushed the door open, the vision before her made her frown and she wondered if they were in the right room. She wandered in a bit, looking around in confusion for the manager. Jay stepped around her surveying the scene.

Behind him, the room was decorated in all black with gold accents, and a lit backdrop flashed the words 'Marry Me'. He grabbed her hands and led her to the center of the room. Stunned, she followed. Her nerves were on ten and she trembled when she began to ascertain what was going on.

"Oh my God," she murmured under her breath, feeling dazed. Tears sprang up in her eyes, again, and her heart was fluttering like a million butterflies were trapped inside it. She looked around again and started to notice little details, like their names printed on the balloons, and their picture on a posterboard mimicking the movie board for *Boomerang*.

From the opposite end of the room, another door opened, and Shane stepped inside followed by Remy, Dom, and Jackson. Behind her, the door opened, and she turned to see Chelle, Joey, Kiko and Mallory, her parents, and his family. Nicole's eyes widened when she saw his grandmother, who had traveled from Jamaica.

"Before you say anything, let me speak," he said. When she nodded, he continued. "I know that you're going to say this is too soon, or that you just got divorced, but we both know none of that matters. If I believed in love at first sight, then I'd say I've loved you since I first saw you practicing your moves in the FAMU gymnasium, and you've been slowly stealing pieces of my heart ever since. I love you so much it doesn't even make any sense, but there's nothing I wouldn't do for you, Nicole. So, this ring," he paused to pull an iconic Tiffany blue ring box out of his pocket and lowered down on one knee.

One hand flew to her face and the other covered her heart as if she was trying to hold her surprise in.

"This ring is a symbol of my commitment to you. It doesn't have to be today, tomorrow, or even next year, but you're going to be my wife. I've been trying to tell you, so now here's the proof. Nicole Angel Brown, will you marry me?"

"Yes," she cried. Her immediate response surprised him, and he sagged in relief. His own tears trickled as the fear that she might reject him seeped out.

Nicole bent down and threw her arms around him. It was too soon, and she *had* just gone through a divorce, but the time they had spent apart taught her a valuable lesson. She wasn't going to throw love away because it didn't make sense. All that mattered was that her heart beat for Jay, and she loved every bit of the man he was. No one was ever going to come close.

For a moment it felt like they were in their own world, until the claps and cheers from their family and friends began to register. Jay straightened his back, slid the ring on her finger and stood. The look of genuine love that flowed between them could be seen by everyone in the room. Then he cradled her face, admiring her beauty, tears and all, before sealing his promise with a kiss.

Someone popped a bottle of champagne and then Chelle was calling for a toast as they were bombarded with hugs and congratulations from their loved ones. Mr. and Mrs. Brown were ecstatic and rained down praise and prayers over the couple. Nicole was overwhelmed with the outpouring of love and began to ugly cry. A pair of soft arms with a familiar spicy floral scent wrapped around her.

"It's ok bestie. We won't love you any less for being so soft," Kiko whispered against her cheek before she kissed it. Nicole chuckled, hugging her back fiercely. Of course, Chelle and Joey joined them making it a group hug.

"I love y'all," Nicole sniffed as her crying began to subside.
"We love you right back," Chelle said.
"Yes, we do, but we're glad you said yes because we were gonna have to jump you if you didn't," Joey stated, and they all burst out laughing.

Around the room, waiters were distributing champagne glasses as music began to play. "Girl Of My Dreams" by Keith Sweat was the first song on the DJ list, and Nicole recognized it as a song that Jay played all the time. She searched for him, finding him on the other side of the room with Shane and Kelly, and their eyes locked. He raised his glass to her as her father called for quiet as he made the first toast.

"I'm not a man of many words," he started causing everyone to chuckle because he was known for always speaking his mind. "But all a father wants for his daughter is for her to find a man who he respects and can entrust her to. Someone who will love her and take care of her the same way you would. I am proud to be able to do that today. Jay, God bless you."

There was a smattering of chuckles from those who caught the double entendre, and then a round of applause. Then, their friends gathered for a hilarious group toast about all the couple's antics over the years and what each of them saw that hinted of them being together someday. Nicole felt the emotion tightening her throat as she processed the enormity of it all.

Glancing around the room at the other couples, she was still trying to grasp that not only were she and Jay official, but they were engaged. She watched her parents, her ultimate relationship goals, and was proud that she could finally live up to their example. Chelle was with Remy, Kiko was with Dom, Joey was with Dante, and Shane was with Kelly. It was surreal that they were all growing up and settling down.

"Soon As I Get Home" began to play, and Jay pulled Nicole onto the dance floor. When he had sung it to her at karaoke, she had no idea just how true his words were. She settled into his arms, and he rested his chin on top of her head as they rocked back and forth.

"I'm so surprised you didn't give me a hard time," he said.
"I guess I'm turning over a new leaf," she replied.
"Shit. Well, I'm glad you started with me."

"Shut up," she chuckled.

He pulled back to look into her eyes as he caressed her cheek.

"Are you happy?"

His concern touched her, and she vowed to make him feel as loved and seen as he made her.

"I love you," she declared, prepared for the kiss that ensued. It had been an implied concept up until that point, and she needed him to know how real it was.

"Don't ever leave me again," he said, his eyes sober.
"I won't," she replied.
"Promise?"
"Promise," she agreed with a kiss.

The sun shone brightly down on Nicole and Chelle as they lunched on the outdoor patio of the Mandarin Garden Restaurant. They both sipped on Crodinos as they waited to settle their bill.
"Can you charge it to my room, please?" Nicole asked in a crude translation of Italian.
"Si, signora," their server replied with a smile that widened as she handed him a tip in Italian

Lira.

"Wow, you're getting better," Chelle remarked.

"Girl, I'm trying. If we're going to be here for another two years, I have to."

"If we had known you guys were gonna love it so much, Remy could have negotiated a longer contract instead of that provisional one-year deal."

"I know," Nicole agreed. "It doesn't even feel like we've been here for a year. Even though I miss you guys like crazy, I'm loving it here."

After the surprise engagement, the couple had a serious conversation about their future and what that looked like. Jay was prepared to forgo any career in basketball and focus on being a businessman, but Nicole shocked him by agreeing to move if that's what he wanted. She had returned to Europe with him to complete his try out circuit and fell in love with Italy. So, when their team offered him a spot on the roster, he took it.

Worried about how things would play out, he didn't want to sign a lengthy contract, and Remy, in his first official role as an agent, was able to work out a one-year deal. Now that it was almost up, both Jay and the Italian team were interested in renewing, so Remy and Chelle flew out to process the deal.

"But look at you and Remy being the dynamic duo," Nicole said. "Who would have thought?"

"Who would have thought, indeed. We were

practically mortal enemies at one point."

"More like fake enemies," Nicole said and rolled her eyes.

"Oh please. Like you weren't harboring secret feelings for Jay. All that time you spent acting like you couldn't stand him!"

"I couldn't stand him," Nicole chuckled.

"Yeah, 'cause you couldn't *have* him," Chelle sassed.

"Oh, I could have had him. I was just too busy being loyal."

"Well, I won't hold that against you."

"Thank you, friend," Nicole grinned. "I'm just sad Kiko couldn't make it."

"I know. Dommy Jr. was sick, and she was afraid the flight would make it worse. You know, with the air pressure."

"Yeah. Poor thing almost cried when she found out babies can get earaches from flying."

"Who knew Kiko would be *that* mommy?"

"I know!" Nicole laughed. "But I love to see it."

"Well since you'll be here a little longer, we'll just have to plan something."

"Yeah. Shane is coming as soon as the NBA season is over."

"Yeah, his team isn't making it to the playoffs this year. It sucks, because he loves Phoenix, but he's probably not going to stay there," Chelle said.

"Oh really? So where would he go next?"

"Interestingly enough, L.A. is looking at him." Chelle raised her brows and Nicole got the drift.

"Interesting indeed. Also interesting is that Joey is planning to come around the same time," Nicole added.

"No comment," Chelle grinned.

Nicole's phone dinged with a text. "Let me go. I want to get Jay's bath ready for when he comes in. Helps him relax after practice."

"Now who knew you'd be such a good little wifey?" Chelle teased her.

"Jay, "Nicole said, sticking out her tongue.

"Alright. I gotta go review this contract. I'll see you tonight for dinner."

Nicole went up to their suite and slipped off her clothes. She looked forward to the after-practice baths as much as Jay, because she got in the tub with him. She would massage his tired limbs, and more times than not they'd end up in bed. Opening her bedside table, she pulled out the paper bag that had been sitting there since that morning. She wanted everything to be ready for when he came in.

Walking into the bathroom, she turned the brass knob for the hot water then the cold, sitting on the side of the tub as the sound of the rushing water lulled her into deep thought. Getting married wasn't something they were rushing to do, but she had been thinking a lot about it lately. So many things had changed in the previous year, and she wondered what that meant for their future.

The heavy door of their hotel room slammed closed, announcing Jay's return. He stalked into the bathroom, his eyes searching for her, holding the paper bag in his hand.

"Hey," he said with a warm smile when he saw her already half naked. "What's this?" He waved the bag at her.

"Why don't you open it," she said, smiling extra sweetly.

With a suspicious glance, Jay opened the bag and pulled out a pregnancy test. The two lines were a deep pink, signaling a strong positive. Jay grinned, putting the test back in the bag and tossing it on the counter.

"It's about time," he said.

"Huh?" Nicole was expecting to surprise him, but he simply started undressing for his bath like it wasn't a big deal.

"I've known you were pregnant for a few weeks," he replied.

"What? How did you know?" She was completely befuddled.

"For starters, your period was super light last month, and late or probably not coming this month," he explained.

"Wow, ok."

"And," he stepped toward her, reaching his hand

out to slip her bra strap over her shoulder and down her arm until he revealed one of her breasts. When he groped her, she moaned and shuddered under his touch.

"You're so sensitive," he murmured as he leaned forward and flicked his tongue over her nipple, while slipping a finger into her panties that were already soaked. "Your pussy has never been this wet. All the time. I can't even think straight anymore."

Nicole groaned as he slid his middle finger inside her while continuing to plump and tease her breast. She had suspected something was off when her normally heavy period was barely a blip that lasted a couple of days. Then the horniness set in, and she thought she was losing her mind. When she missed her period the previous week, she knew something was up. The fact that he already knew was comical, but also so much like Jay.

He knew her better than she knew her damn self.

The End

One Last Thing...

If you enjoyed this book, I'd be very grateful if you'd post a short review on Amazon. Your support really does make a difference and I read all the reviews personally so I can get your feedback and make the next book even better.

Thank you!

About The Author

Olivia Linden is a best-selling author of steamy romance and romantic suspense stories with diverse characters. Her stories mix her big personality with a sexy yet humorous tone, weaving tales of passion and suspense that you can feel; branding you with her unique vibe.Find more of her stories on
Amazon.com

Joing the Olivia Linden Mailing list!

Other Books by Olivia Linden

Jaded Hearts
Only Her Heart
Forever Her Heart
Secret Obsession
Naturally Naughty
Out Of Luck
Forever My Lady